UNRAVELING

REVELATION

Attainable Understanding for Everyone

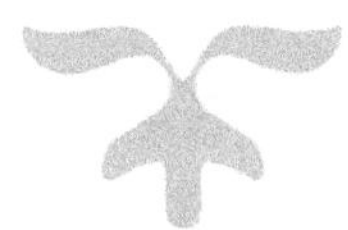

To Suzanne

The delight of my eyes

ACKNOWLEDGMENTS

There are too many people to give credit to for the existence of Unraveling Revelation. Some suffered through my attempts to teach Revelation in Bible class at Lincoln Park Church of Christ in Michigan, including my son Brandon Smith. Then there is Vince Poscente, who didn't know he would help me write this book when he wrote The Ant and the Elephant. I got excellent tips, encouragement, and advice from two prolific authors, Aubrey Johnson and LaGard Smith. The best daughter anyone could ask for, Ginger Hernandez, read my book, gave her encouragement, and helped me design the cover along with Fawcett Publications. My good friend Teresa Wylie read an early draft and helped me make my wording more friendly. Terri is also responsible for the book title. Finally, my dear friend, Farrah Sargent, has been invaluable to me. Farrah's encouragement and suggestions have resulted in significant improvements. Of course, this book could not have been written without the support of my wonderful wife, Suzanne. Space may be the final frontier, but it is also required to write a book. Suzanne has allowed me the space to do so and is a sounding board for my thoughts and frustrations.

CONTENTS

Preface 1

Chapter 1 Method 3

Chapter 2 Alpha 7

Chapter 3 A Wonderful Savior 21

Chapter 4: A Church under Pressure 34

Chapter 5 The Throne of God 50

Chapter 6 The Scroll and Seven Seals 64

Chapter 7 The Seven Trumpets 77

Chapter 8 The Seven-Headed Dragon 95

Chapter 9 The Two Beasts 105

Chapter 10 The Seven Voices 115

Chapter 11 The Seven Bowls 128

Chapter 12 The Prostitute 141

Chapter 13 The Rider 157

Chapter 14 The City of the Victorious 170

Chapter 15 Omega 180

Study Guide 186

End Notes 199

Figures and Tables

Table 1: Numerology of Revelation 16

Table 2 Themes of Revelation 20

Table 3: Son of Man and Ancient of Days 28

Table 4: A Wonderful Savior 33

Table 5: Comparison of the Churches 35

Table 6: Terms and Definitions 47

Table 7: Descriptions of God 63

Table 8: Vision Comparison 106

Table 9: The Description of the 144,000 117

Table 10: Three Representations of God's Judgement 138

Table 11: Comparing the Beasts 142

Figure 1: 1000 Year Symbolism 168

PREFACE

Let me start with one clear statement. Revelation is about one thing and one thing only – heart change.

This is not a commentary. It is, at heart, a gospel message of uplifting encouragement and evangelism. It is, however, written in the style of a commentary to some extent. I am not a scholar. Scholars, by and large, have not helped most people understand Revelation. Some commentaries are more challenging to read than Revelation, and the comments are sometimes too technical for most readers. Another problem commentators have with Revelation is trying to give the reader all possible views of an object or event, leading to confusion.

I think the book of Revelation is the most encouraging and exciting in the Bible. Our world sorely needs this message today. A problem is that people get so overwhelmed by the weird and unfamiliar objects, events, and creatures in Revelation that they lose the message. Another problem is people's focus on their millennial view. A person's millennial view is based on their view of the 1000-year reign spoken of in Revelation 20. Those who believe we live in an era before the millennia are called "Pre-millennials." Those who think we live in an era after the millennia are called "Post-millennials." Those who believe that the 1000-year reign is symbolic of the time in which we currently live are called "Amillennials." This view generally depends on how literally you take the Book of Revelation. This leads to arguments over whether an object or event is a symbol. Often, debates over the interpretation of whether the objects and events are actual or symbolic take the wind out of a person's sails in their effort to capture the message.

These concerns are tangential to the message of Revelation. They are concerns related to the message of Revelation but do not affect the actual message. It doesn't matter if you are Premillennial, Postmillennial, Amillennial, or B millennial; the message of Revelation is still the same — it transcends all those considerations.

There are several methods of interpreting the Book of Revelation. Here are six. By name only: futurists, preterists, apocalyptic, historicists, philosophy of history, and parallelists.[i] Let me assure you that the original readers had no such concerns. Then there are our current concerns about Pre-millennialism, Post-millennialism, or Amillennialism. Again, let me assure you that the first readers never thought of such things. The message of Revelation is far beyond these concerns. Therefore, I will deemphasize these concepts. The critical message is universal. If these ideas concern you, you can determine where I fall on the spectrum by reading this book. However, I don't want those ideas to cloud the message.

Having said all that, I will keep these kinds of discussions to a minimum and highlight what I believe to be the actual message. If you want a detailed description of all the objects, events, and creatures in the book, plenty of books focus on those things.[ii]

Again, I believe that Revelation is about heart change, which motivates behavior change.

Revelation is simple. It explains itself in so many ways. I want to help you remove your fear of the book. As stated above, the primary purpose is to motivate the correct behavior by showing the results of living in rebellion to God in contrast to the results of living in obedience to God and in congruence with his will.

I suggest you have your Bible open and handy as you read this book.

CHAPTER 1

METHOD

Revelation indicates the method it uses to get its point across in the first few verses of chapter 1. John says he testifies to everything he saw. This is a visual revelation. Someone should read it audibly, and others should listen. But the words describe pictures with meaning behind them – they are signs. Those who take the message to heart will receive the blessing the message provides. As we read Revelation, we must carefully imagine the pictures described to us to take them to heart and reshape our lives according to the message.

The parable "The Ant and the Elephant," by Vince Pascente,[III] best describes the method Revelation uses to speak to and change us. This is a parable that describes the way the human mind works. To summarize, when we think consciously, we use the front of our brains to fire about 2000 neurons per second. When we feel subconsciously, which is to say visually and emotionally, we fire about 40 billion neurons per second. So, conscious thought compared to subconscious thought is like comparing the power of an ant to that of an elephant. Subconscious thought has 20,000 times more control over our actions than conscious thought.

If an ant was on the back of an elephant and wanted to go left, but the elephant wanted to go right, which way would the ant go? Right, of course, since it has no power to change the direction of the elephant. We work the same way. I may know that going left is the correct way, but if I have an emotional need to go right, it makes no difference where I should go; I'm going where my emotions take me. Paul describes this condition in Romans 7:14-25 where he talks about wanting to do good things but ending up doing things he did not want to do. Consciously, he would try to do good things but would end up doing things he did not want. This problem of his subconscious mind having different purposes than his conscious mind caused him to want to do one thing but end up doing another.

Pascente presents some strategies in his book about how to use your conscious brain to train your subconscious brain so that when your ant knows that left is the correct direction to go. Your elephant is on the same page and goes left. He teaches that you should use visualization to train your subconscious that what you logically want is right and good. Athletes use this technique to excel at sports. TV uses this technique to get you to buy products. Why not use this technique to get yourself to think the way God wants you to think and to act the way God wants you to act?

Revelation uses pictures to do just that! It uses both positive motivation and negative motivation. We see evil, corrupt government, corrupt religion, and corrupt business as turbulent waters, as the beast, and as all manner of evil things. We see the judgment of such entities in horrific pictures, and it inspires us to move away from the lifestyle supported by those entities. We also see the fantastic throne room scenes, the victory of the great angel, the triumph of Jesus, the marriage feast, and more to inspire us to move toward a godly lifestyle.

You will notice that the number of negative pictures far outweighs the positive. You will also see this principle in Deuteronomy 28, where God spends the first 14 verses telling the Israelites what blessings await them in the promised land if they are faithful and 4 times that many verses warning them about what curses await if they are unfaithful. Why is there so much more judgment than blessings? The answer is that negative inspiration is more effective than positive. Imagine, for example, that it is a beautiful, sunny, 72-degree day, and you want to go out and enjoy the sunshine. You might leave your house because of that positive motivation, but it is no big deal if you don't. However, you realize that your home has become a blazing inferno. Now, there is little that will stop you from getting out of your house. Positive inspiration pulls gently. Negative inspiration pushes violently.

Now consider Ephesians 3:20. Paul says that God can do immeasurably more than all we ask or imagine, according to his power that is at work within us. Revelation teaches the most powerful part of us through visualization. That method involves prayer—asking and imagining what God could do in our lives and through us to spread the glory of his gospel to others.

This is an interactive method by which the message of Revelation works in our lives. We see the turmoil described in Revelation played out daily, and we respond by imagining God doing great and marvelous things in the world and taking these things to him in prayer. As we said in the preface, Revelation is about heart change. Much of that heart change comes about by humbly taking things to God in prayer and expecting that God hears our prayers. We must not overlook the fact that the prayers of the saints prompt the events pictured in Revelation.[IV]

Revelation only mentions prayer twice; both times, it is with incense. In 5:6-9, Jesus has center stage. Those who are worshipping are offering him prayers and incense. In 8:1-5, prayers and incense have center stage while the angel is offering them on the altar. The altar is where God's throne is facing. It is the center of God's focus. The prayers of the saints are a sweet, wonderful smell to God. He cherishes our prayers!

We must invest time in God's word and prayer, imagining what he can do in and through us, your local congregation, and the whole church. We are not powerless to change this world. We must get our imaginations going, followed up with goals and actions, to see God carry out His vision for us in His world.

So, as we study Revelation, we must use our conscious mind to try to understand the pictures we see and as many details of the symbolism as we can. There are also sections, especially chapters 2 and 3, which speak more to the conscious mind than the subconscious. But we must not lose ourselves trying to understand every detail of the tree leaves we risk not seeing the forest. An example of some details that I will not get caught up in is in Revelation 21:19-20. Here, John sees the 12 foundations of New Jerusalem. Each of the city's foundations has a decoration with a different precious stone, and Revelation lists them by name. Spending time determining what each stone symbolizes or if they represent anything is a mistake. The point is that they are each precious, valuable, and unique. We must not focus so much on ant food that we do not feed the elephant. Feeding the elephant will get us where we want to go.

CHAPTER 2

ALPHA

Revelation 1:1 to 1:4.

John introduces the book of Revelation in the first four verses. We can learn a lot about this book, its source, how it is constructed, and how it will be used in these verses.

1:1 The revelation from Jesus Christ, which God gave him to show his servants what must soon take place. He made it known by sending his angel to his servant John. 2, who testifies to everything he saw—that is, the word of God and the testimony of Jesus Christ. 3 Blessed is the one who reads aloud the words of this prophecy, and blessed are those who hear it and take to heart what is written in it because the time is near. 4 John, To the seven churches in the province of Asia...

TECHNICALITIES

Let us get some technical issues out of the way before we begin. The accepted author of Revelation is John, one of the original 12 disciples of Jesus, whom he called to be apostles. John is also the gospel's author, bearing his name and three letters: 1 John, 2 John, and 3 John. There is good scholarship calculating that John wrote Revelation around A.D. 95.[v] There is also good scholarship dating the writing of Revelation to before A.D. 70.[vi] Very respectable people have changed their minds about the date of the writing. I confess that I find arguments for both dates acceptable, but I have favored the A.D. 95 date in my writing.

This is apocalyptic literature, meaning visions and symbols reveal the message. Of course, this scares many people away from studying the book. We can spend too much time figuring out what everything means word-by-word rather than focusing on the text's message, which is the fascinating part of the book.

Let us read this naturally, just like we were reading a letter we received from someone. Imagine you are living some 2000 years ago and reading this or hearing it read to you for the first time. This is how we must read any literature produced so long ago. We must consider how the original recipients would have understood the message.

THE COMMISSION

John was commissioned to bear testimony to Jesus, as we see in verse 2. The very reason John found himself in exile on the island of Patmos, the location from which he was writing, was *because* of the word of God and the testimony of Jesus (1:9, italics mine). The apostles, of whom John was a member, and the angels are all servants who *hold* to the testimony of Jesus (19:10, italics mine). The Spirit of God inspires prophecy, which bears testimony to Jesus. Therefore, we worship God!

John's commission was to write to the seven churches. First, an angel was sent to John to make a revelation known to him, as we see in 1:1. But then, in verse 11, we will see that John is ordered (authorized or given the mission) to write down the things he would see. He sent these things to seven churches, all of which were in what is now known as Asia Minor. There were more than seven churches in the area, however. An example is Colossae, to whom the Book of Colossians was written in the Bible. Why was this message commissioned to only seven churches? As noted in the section below on numerology, seven represents completeness or fullness. These seven churches represent the complete church. These churches' individual characteristics will appear throughout the age until Jesus returns. We can look at these churches, compare them to the church we attend, follow their encouragement, and heed the warnings against them. As a high school math teacher, a friend of mine once pointed out, "A teaching technique is when you have five students misbehaving, you call out one of them, and they all straighten up." Therefore, Revelation has a general message for all. This is why God warns us not to add to or take away from the message of Revelation.[VII]

FOLLOW THE MONEY!

It is important to look at the source of things. How many times have you heard "follow the money" in a movie, in politics, or in business? If you want to know why something is happening, follow the money that is funding the event, and that will lead you to the source and the motivation for the event. In many industries, tracking the lineage of materials is important for quality control. If something goes bad in food or medicine, the manufacturers can go to the batch, know the exact source of all the components or ingredients, and quarantine the necessary products. John assures us that Revelation was not something he produced on his own by giving us the source of his message.

These first four verses give us the lineage of the material presented in the Revelation. *The revelation from Jesus Christ, which God gave him ... He made it known by sending his angel to his servant John ... John, To the seven churches in the province of Asia...*

We have received the revelation because John wrote it to seven churches in the province of Asia. They received it from John, who received it from an angel, who received it from Jesus, who received it from God. God himself is the very source of the message that we are receiving from John! It is trustworthy! It is true! We know that God cannot lie, and he is always consistent with himself. So, we know the message of Revelation is reliable and true, good and right.

As J.B. Coffman noted, "All true knowledge of God comes from God, and even that conveyed by the blessed Savior himself came from the Father."[VIII] That is what we see here in Revelation 1:1-3. Coffman also notes that Peter's confession about Jesus' identity was not revealed to him by "flesh and blood" but by "the Father in heaven[IX]." This is why this chain of evidence appears in Revelation.

But could not God have given the revelation directly to John? Why such a long handing-off of the message from God to the churches? Interestingly, this chain of evidence closely mimics the process of when the law was given to Moses. In Paul's letter to the Galatians,[X] we read that "...*the law was given through angels and entrusted to a mediator.*" God gave the law to the Israelites by Moses, the mediator. However, Paul says that Moses did not get the law directly from God but through angels. In like manner, John did not receive the revelation directly from God but through angels.

The purpose of Paul's statement in Galatians is to contrast how Moses received the law with how Abraham received the promises. Abraham received this promise directly from God: "All peoples on earth will be blessed through you." That promise still stands, but the law was temporary. The law was given at the inception of the nation of Israel, some 430 years after the promise was given, and it was removed when Christ came.[XI]

THE TIME IS NEAR

Does this mean that Revelation has a limited scope, as did the law? Certainly, the law is different from Revelation. The law was made up of commands that the Israelites must follow to bring them to Christ. Revelation 1:1 tells us that we are being shown "*what must soon take place.*" We see this immediately repeated in verse 3, where we are told that "*the time is near.*" This is repeated at least eight more times in Revelation.[XII]

The time is near. For what? What, exactly, must soon take place? The context of each of these statements may be different, and we need to be aware of that. For instance, 11:14 says, "The second woe is passed; the third woe is coming soon." The point here is that the third woe is coming shortly after the second woe. Therefore, the time is only near for the third woe in reference to the time of the completion of the second woe.

Another thing to consider is that John is telling us that things will begin soon after his writing. That does not necessarily speak of the completion of the events. I may say that I will soon start a project, but that does not indicate when the project will be completed. It could be a two-week project, a two-year project, or a two-millennia project.

Revelation 22:10 may add some interesting insight into this. It says: Then he (the angel) told me (John), "*Do not seal up the words of the prophecy of this scroll, because the time is near.*" This reminds me of Daniel 8:26, where Daniel was told to "*seal up the vision, for it concerns the distant future.*" Commentators agree that Daniel 8 speaks of Antiochus Epiphanes, who reigned from about 171 BC to 165 BC. Daniel wrote this around 550 BC, some 380 years before the events, yet he is told it is the distant future. In contrast, John is told *not* to seal the prophecy because the time is near. If the same God says to Daniel that something that happens 380 years in the future is the distant future and later says to John that the time is near, does that not imply that the events that John is relating must have been completed within 380 years?

What is my point in this observation? Many people suggest that the events depicted in Revelation are about the fall of Rome or have not yet happened. According to historians, Rome fell in 476 AD. If, as we asserted, Revelation was written in AD 95, that is a difference of 380 years. How could 380 years both be the distant future for Daniel and soon for the seven churches? Even more dramatically, if the events of Revelation haven't happened yet, how could nearly 2000 years be considered soon?

As it is our method of discovering these things as we read the book, we must keep these questions in mind.

SHOW TIME

Still, in verse 1, we are told that the revelation was "to show his servants" what must soon take place, and in verse 2, John assures us that he *"testifies to everything he saw."* The word "show" is used eight times throughout the book. The word "saw," as in "I saw," is used 42 times, and the word "seen," as in "have seen," is used 16 times! That is a total of 66 uses of words that point us toward the seeing of things.

This is a visual revelation – indeed, the very nature of apocalyptic literature is that of a message being delivered through visions. It is expressed in words, but we are called to visualize what John saw. The power of visualization has been documented in every area of life. The athlete visualizes her victory before she performs. The businessperson visualizes a successful meeting before the meeting begins. The inventor visualizes his invention before the work starts. The builder visualizes the tower or bridge before the work begins. There is power in visualization that does not exist in mere words.

That which we visualize or imagine bypasses the logical mind and goes directly for the heart and our emotions. Logical thought has extraordinarily little power to motivate. Our emotions impact our actions ten million times more than logical thought. When our emotions are involved, we are motivated to act with a power that is simply lost to logic. The purpose of visualizing the things revealed in Revelation is to motivate us through our emotions to run from evil and run toward righteousness. We will see this play out repeatedly throughout the book of Revelation.

What is it that John saw? Verse two says he saw ... *the word of God and the testimony of Jesus Christ*. How does one see the "word of God" or the "testimony of Jesus Christ"? Based on John 1:1-18, the word of God refers to Jesus himself. So that was not too hard, but what about the "testimony of Jesus Christ"? Jesus is testifying, giving testimony to those things which must soon take place. The events that were soon to occur for the recipients of the revelation were being revealed to them visually.

A BLESSING

Revelation involves a blessing. Seven blessings are listed, giving the impression of being completely blessed. Verse 3 has the first blessing.

Blessed is the one who reads aloud the words of this prophecy, and blessed are those who hear it and take to heart what is written in it because the time is near.

There are two criteria for receiving the blessing spoken of here. The first is that you either read the prophecy aloud or hear it read. The second is that you take it to heart. Notice that we are again bypassing the logical mind and heading right for the heart. God's purpose of the revelation is to aim for the heart! He wants the heart to change! That is where the true blessing of revelation resides: in a changed heart.

Much of what is written about Revelation is centered on the cerebral. Much ink is spent trying to describe what all the details mean rather than discovering what message God is trying to get burnt into our hearts. Do not get me wrong; we will certainly discuss the meaning of many details, but my goal is to determine how those details relate to the heart message. So, the meaning of an item is only important in relation to the greater message that is being shared.

There is yet an even more serious reason that God is trying to get this message to the heart of the first-century churches—the happenings described in the revelation will soon be experienced by the churches. They need to be prepared to act so that they come out on the right side of the persecutions and trials that are to take place.

So where is the blessing in that? There is certainly a blessing in going into persecution, knowing the true nature of the persecutors, the persecution, the end of the persecutors, the end of those who succumb to persecution, and the end of those who persevere and are victorious. Those being persecuted would need all the tools available to stand firm through the trials they were about to face so that whether they live or die, they would be blessed with an eternal life of heavenly joy in their heavenly home. Paul spoke of this very thing in his second letter to the church in Thessalonica. Please read 2 Thessalonians 1:3-10. John gives us a visual picture of what Paul expresses there. Our view of suffering becomes one of joy when we understand that our patient endurance proves that God's judgment is right and that we are rewarded with the worthiness of the kingdom of God. Patient endurance of suffering produces wonderful things in us.

MORE BLESSINGS

One of the most important themes of Revelation is the seven blessings.

1:3 *Blessed is the one who reads aloud the words of this prophecy, and blessed are those who hear it and take to heart what is written in it because the time is near.*

14:13 *Then I heard a voice from heaven say, "Write this: Blessed are the dead who die in the Lord from now on." "Yes," says the Spirit, "they will rest from their labor, for their deeds will follow them."*

16:15 *"Look, I come like a thief! Blessed is the one who stays awake and remains clothed so as not to go naked and be shamefully exposed."*

19:9 *Then the angel said to me, "Write this: Blessed are those who are invited to the wedding supper of the Lamb!" And he added, "These are the true words of God."*

20:6 *Blessed and holy are those who share in the first resurrection. The second death has no power over them, but they will be priests of God and of Christ and will reign with him for a thousand years.*

22:7 *"Look, I am coming soon! Blessed is the one who keeps the words of the prophecy written in this scroll."*

22:14 *"Blessed are those who wash their robes, that they may have the right to the tree of life and may go through the gates into the city.*

Isn't this wonderful? I am sure you want these blessings as I do! John said that the test for whether we would receive these blessings was to read the message aloud and take what is written there to heart. We must realize that there is a third test as well. Since we are so far removed from the culture, events, and lifestyle that the seven churches of Asia were facing in the first century, we must take some time and effort to obtain the message we are to receive. This reminds me of one of my favorite quotes:

The task must be made difficult, for only the difficult inspires the noble-hearted.

-Danish philosopher Soren Kierkegaard

I pray that we will be shown to be noble-hearted and inspired by that which is difficult. God wants us to experience these blessings, too. It is not too hard for us to understand. This is a book of encouragement, blessing, and hope for the faithful.

NUMEROLOGY

The concept of numerology is important in Jewish literature, especially apocalyptic literature. Many commentaries and other sources provide details about numerology, so I'll summarize some of the numbers and their meanings here.

Table 1: Numerology of Revelation

Two: The number of witnesses to make a testimony valid.

Three: This refers to the divine, to that which is heavenly, to God. For example, there is the Father, Son, and Holy Spirit. There are three beings in the godhead, but they are intricately linked as one deity. Another example is found in Isaiah 6:3, where the Lord is called "Holy, Holy, Holy." This does not refer to his 3-in-1 nature but means he is Holy to the max!

Four: This refers to creation, as in the four corners of the earth. Humans are also fourfold, having a physical being, an emotional being, a mental being, and a spiritual being. These four parts are intricately linked into one human being, just as the Father, Son and Holy Spirit are linked into one deity.

Seven: Fullness, completeness, or perfection.

Six: One short of seven. It does not measure up. Six is the number of man.

PROPHECY

Prophecy does not necessarily refer to the telling of future events. Rather, it signifies "the speaking forth of the mind and counsel of God,' [XIII] and "the gift of communicating and enforcing revealed truth." [XIV]

The word, Prophecy, is used only 6 times in Revelation. In 19:10, John falls down to worship an angel who tells him, "Don't do that!" This verse ends with representing the trinity. Worship God, not a created being; The Spirit brings prophecy; The prophecy bears testimony to Jesus! God is completely united in all his work!

In 22:10, John is told, "Don't seal up," in 22:18 we are all told, "Don't add to," and in 22:19, we are all told, "Don't remove from" the words of this prophecy. We can be guilty of sealing up the prophecy by never reading it, by interpreting it out of context with the rest of scripture, by adding to it, or by subtracting from it. Each of these actions will nullify or make scripture void (cf. Mark 7:8-13). Let us not do those things!

In Revelation, we are told that there is a blessing in keeping and applying the prophecy to our lives.[XV] Let us do that!

MYSTERY

In the ordinary sense, a 'mystery' implies knowledge withheld; its Scriptural significance is that truth is revealed.[XVI] In the Bible, a 'mystery' is not something unknowable. Rather, it is what can only be known through revelation, i.e., because God reveals it. [XVII]

The word "mystery" is used four times in the Revelation.[XVIII] In each case, indeed, every time this word is used in the New Testament, the mystery is revealed to us.

REVELATION

Finally, Revelation. This word is used only once in Revelation – in the first verse. It is principally used for the revelation of Jesus Christ (the Word), especially a particular (spiritual) manifestation of Christ (His will) previously unknown to the extent (because "veiled, covered"). [XIX]

Also, it is defined as "a surprising and previously unknown fact, especially one that is made known in a dramatic way." This is certainly an apt description of the way things are revealed in Revelation.

Now, back to verse 3. John says, "Blessed (happy) are those who read aloud or hear the words of the prophecy and take it to heart because the time is near." Here are some questions we want to answer as we study through the book.

1. Why might the original recipient have been happy about the message of Revelation?

2. Do we find ourselves in similar situations?

3. Are we assured of the same kind of encouragement that they had? How?

SUFFERING

Those who suffer, in Revelation, are predominantly those who are faithful to God. It becomes clear throughout the book that God is aware of the suffering of his faithful people. His encouragement is that this takes patient endurance. If God's people continue to be faithful to Jesus, keep his commands, and endure patiently, we are assured rest from our labors. There is, however, a hint early on, in 2:22, that suffering is going to move from the faithful to the faithless. But that leads us to the next theme, which is judgment. [xx]

JUDGMENT

Those who suffer are crying out to God, "When will you judge those who have caused all this trouble in our lives!?" God assures his holy people who have suffered so much that the perpetrators of evil will be judged.

In Revelation 16:15, Jesus warns us that he will come like a thief. This reminds us of 1 Thessalonians 5:2, where the church is told that Jesus would come like a thief in the night for those who are not awake and alert and looking for him. It will certainly be a surprise for the faithful, but it will also be a welcome surprise and a day of rejoicing, relief, and love. The church is told in 1 Thessalonians 5:4-11 that we are not in darkness, so this day should surprise us like a thief in the night. This is true because we remain sober, have put faith and love on a breastplate, and have the hope of salvation as a helmet protecting our heads. Therefore, be encouraged and encourage others.

The apostle Peter also warned us that the day of the Lord will come like a thief. See this in 2 Peter 3, especially verses 10-13. He makes it clear that when Jesus returns, there will be nothing left. The final day of judgment will have come. But his main point is that this day is delayed for a particularly good reason. That being that God does not want anyone to perish! He wants to give everyone a chance to repent. What could be more encouraging than that?

Unfortunately, many will persist in unbelief and abuse of those who have put their faith and hope in God. They will suffer the judgment that is being made ready for them. But even that leads us to the final theme, the worship of an awesome God. [XXI]

WORSHIP OF AN AWESOME GOD

First, we see in Revelation 4:8-11 the worship of the four living creatures representing the whole of creation. They are joined by the 24 elders representing the people of God in both the Mosaic age and the Christian age. God is Holy, Holy, Holy! Then, in 5:9-14, these same beings are seen worshiping the Lamb, and they are joined by the angels and every living creature everywhere. I hope you will spend some time with these references and allow your heart to swell with the worship of such an awesome God. Allow yourself to be drawn to him and yourself to be raised toward his likeness.

We see that the book of Revelation is really a book of blessings, hope, and joy! Like Rev 14:12, this calls for patient endurance and perseverance of the saints, but if we do so, we will be blessed. [XXII]

Table 2 Themes of Revelation

1. Blessing & Happiness - seven blessings.
2. Suffering.
3. Judgement.
4. Worship of an awesome God.
5. Hope – a sure hope of salvation and a home in heaven.
6. Victory of Christ and his church as seen through the destruction of Babylon.
7. God is in control and will bring his purposes to completion.
8. We can trust God – He knows those who are his, and he can care for them.
9. Excitement – of seeing God work in the world.
10. Glory – for those who are in Christ.
11. The free will of all people to be a part of all these great blessings.

CHAPTER 3

A WONDERFUL SAVIOR

Revelation is a book to be felt more than thought. The images are to go right for the heart, the feeling center of our life that drives action. It is guided by thought and truth but centered on emotion. The emotion elicited by Revelation drives spiritual hunger. In the human psyche, hunger is built by having something scary to run from and something wonderful and beautiful to run toward. Revelation sets up the scary things, evil, to run from and the wonderful and beautiful things, righteousness, to run toward. It does this in pictures – in describing the things that John saw.

BLESSING

1:4 John to the seven churches that are in Asia: Grace to you and peace from him who is and who was and who is to come, and from the seven spirits who are before his throne. 5; and from Jesus Christ, the faithful witness, the firstborn of the dead, and the ruler of kings on earth.

As we transition from the letter's introduction to verses 4 and 5, John wishes the blessing of grace and peace to be upon the seven churches receiving the letter. It has been said that true peace can only follow God's grace! Here, we see that the Trinity is the source of grace and peace. The Father is described as The Immortal One – he who is, who was, and who is to come. Scripture doesn't specify it here, but the Father is on the throne. The Holy Spirit is described as the seven spirits or the sevenfold Spirit. Remember that seven represents fullness, completeness, and unity. The sevenfold Spirit is before the throne – God is reaching out through his Spirit to those around his throne! Jesus Christ is described as the faithful witness, the firstborn from the dead, and the ruler of the kings of the earth. He sits at God's right hand.[XXIII] All these descriptions give you a feeling of ancient power emanating from the throne area, not just of power but also of awesome, indescribable, and immense love.

Jesus is the *faithful witness*. He came to earth and lived out a life of perfect faith in relation to God and his purpose on earth. He perfectly revealed to us everything we can understand about God, His plan and desire for our lives, His invitation to a home in heaven, His awesome love, and His desire for sweet communion with each of us. That is why we can put our faith and trust in Jesus to carry us to heaven as we imitate him, knowing that he will also be the faithful witness of our obedience to him before his Father. And so, he is the faithful witness to us and to his father. I'm sure that there is a lot more to Jesus' faithful witness than this, but take the time to let this into your heart and be amazed by God's love for us and Jesus' faithfulness to him and us.

Jesus is the *firstborn from the dead*. He was not the first one to rise from the dead, but he is the only one, so far, to rise from the dead, never to die again.

Jesus is the *ruler of the kings of the earth*. Just because kings are under Jesus' rule does not mean they do things according to his will. Do I always do things according to the will of those who rule over me? No. It does mean they will have to answer him. That will not be a good day for many rulers.

The promise of grace and peace comes from this Great God, represented by three beings, Father, Spirit, and Son – Jesus. As we saw above, three represents divinity. The Father is represented by three timeframes, resulting in eternity. Sevenfold Spirit for fullness and completeness. The Son, Jesus, is represented by descriptions that are significant for us. This divine, eternal being wants us to have grace and peace. Let's not miss it. Let's be people to whom he is willing to send these gifts. We have a choice. The purpose of Revelation is to motivate that kind of living.

HYMNS OF PRAISE

1:5(b) To him who loves us and has freed us from our sins by his blood. 6; And made us a kingdom, priests to his God and Father, to him be glory and dominion forever and ever. Amen. 7; Behold, he is coming with the clouds, and every eye will see him, even those who pierced him, and all tribes of the earth will wail on account of him. Even so. Amen. 8; "I am the Alpha and the Omega," says the Lord God, "Who is and who was and who is to come, the Almighty."

Following the blessing are two hymns of praise. The first begins in the middle of verse 5 and ends with verse 6. The second is contained in verse 7. Both are giving praise to our Lord, Jesus. The first hymn praises Jesus because of his attitude toward us and what he has done for us. First, He loves us! He. Loves. Me. The creator of the universe loves me. How do I know this? He has freed me (released me NASB) from my sins. How did he do that? By his blood. The creator of the universe set me free by his blood. Is that not worthy of praise? Is that not worthy of my complete adoration? Is that not worthy of my whole life and total obedience? Yes, it is.

Now that we have been freed from our sins, Jesus has made us into a kingdom. By their baptism into his death, those who are his subjects are members of his kingdom. Each subject of his kingdom, male or female, Jew or Gentile, slave or free, rich or poor, he has made into priests. This is our current situation. Each of us is of the royal class and the priestly class. In the Old Covenant, you could only be in one class. A priest could not be a king, and a king could not be a priest. Jesus was the first to fill both roles. He has enabled us to fill both roles. We are royal priests. And for what purpose? To serve his God and Father! Jesus did all of this not for his own glory, not so we would serve him, but so that we would glorify and serve his Father. Yet because of this superb example of self-sacrifice, we shout together, "To Jesus be glory and power forever and ever! Amen."

Please understand that this is not some future reality. Those who are in Christ are now, at this present time, priests in His kingdom. Here are some other verses from scripture that emphasize the point of Revelation 1:6. In verse 9, John says that he is their companion in the suffering and *kingdom* and patient endurance presently. Peter tells his readers in 1 Peter 2:9, "But you are a chosen people, *a royal priesthood*, a holy nation, a people for God's own possession, so that you may proclaim the excellencies of Him who has called you out of darkness into His marvelous light" (NASB). Paul tells the Colossians in Colossians 1:13-14, "For He rescued us from the domain of darkness and transferred us to the *kingdom* of His beloved Son, in whom we have redemption, the forgiveness of sins" (NASB). The kingdom is now. Not some future event. It is here. It is now. (All italics mine).

But verse 7 gives us a vision of the time of the very end, echoing Acts 1:9-11. This verse does not speak of those things which "must soon take place" (vs 1) and of which the "time is near" (vs 3). It is speaking of Jesus' glory and how he will be perceived when he does return at the end of time. To understand end-time events completely, you want to study clear doctrine on this matter, not symbolic language. See 1 Thessalonians 4:13 through 5:11 and 2 Peter 3:10-13. 1 Corinthians 15 is good too. Read Stafford North's book "Like a Thief in the Night,"[XXIV] which explains these scriptures well. For now, all verse 7 tells us is that Jesus will come with the clouds, as he is also described in Daniel 7:13. And as the disciples saw him leave as described in Acts 1:9-11. At that time, everyone will see him, including those who caused his death! Everyone will mourn, even those who are saved by him because we all caused his death. Some will mourn because they are lost eternally; others will mourn for grief that they contributed to the death of their Lord and Savior. But for the second group, that mourning will be turned to joy!

Jesus declares himself to be the Alpha and Omega, the first and the last, the beginning and the end. This is confirmed to be Jesus in Revelation 22:12-13. He can say this because he shares the traits of God, the Father. He is now; he was before time began, and he will continue to be after time is brought to fulfillment. He is The Almighty! What could be more comforting and encouraging for a person going through deep persecution with no end in sight? Knowing that there will be an end and even if you lose your life because of persecution, there is victory in store for you because your life is in the hands of one who is beyond time, beyond the events of this earth. He has you in his care. What can man do to you?

JOHN'S COMMISSION

1:9, I, John, your brother and partner in the tribulation and the kingdom and the patient endurance that are in Jesus, was on the island called Patmos on account of the word of God and the testimony of Jesus. 10, I was in the Spirit on the Lord's Day, and I heard behind me a loud voice like a trumpet. 11, Saying, "Write what you see in a book and send it to the seven churches, to Ephesus and to Smyrna and to Pergamum and to Thyatira and to Sardis and to Philadelphia and to Laodicea."

Now, John is ready to get into it, so he first relates to his readers. He is their brother. He is their partner. He is their companion. We know that he is an apostle, as is so richly displayed in his first letter, where he also refers to his readers as dear children.[xxv] He is also the elder, as he describes himself at the beginning of his second and third letters. In each letter, as here in Revelation, he makes an emotional connection with his readers. Not only is this a hero of the faith, our apostle, and elder, but he is our friend, parent, and brother. More than that, he is our partner and companion in this earthly experience. He has empathy for all the trials that the readers were experiencing, so we can feel the comfort of that empathy coming through John's letters and this Revelation to us even today.

John's companionship with his audience involved three things. They are tribulation or suffering, the kingdom, and patient endurance. These are all ours in Jesus. That's when you say, "What was that now? I'm okay being a subject in God's kingdom. That sounds nice. But I'm not so excited about this suffering and patient endurance stuff. What's that all about?" Please understand that whether you are in Christ or not, you will suffer on this earth. The nature of your suffering may certainly be different, but you will have to suffer something because that is the nature of being human on a fallen earth. The only way to really have patient endurance in your suffering is to have the long view, which only genuinely exists in Christ. Knowing that whatever happens to you on earth, as long as you remain faithful to Christ, you will be able to enjoy your reward in heaven. We remember the Lord's own words, as recorded by this very apostle in his gospel, John 16:33, that because Jesus has overcome the world and we are in him, we can take heart because he has overcome the world. What joy we can have because we are in his kingdom. And we are in his kingdom now while we are on this earth. We don't have to wait for some future time, some 1000-year reign, or when we're in heaven. Jesus' kingdom is real right now.

Now, John is experiencing banishment to the island of Patmos because of his witness to the word of God and the testimony he maintained about Jesus. But, on the Lord's Day, he worships in the Spirit. Nothing keeps a faithful Christian from worshipping the Lord as we are called to do. But unlike most worship services, he hears a loud voice like a trumpet giving him his commission. Imagine hearing a loud voice behind you that sounds like a trumpet. Certainly, you would jump out of your skin! Trumpets were used as signaling devices in battle. Today, they are used for fanfare and pieces that project power. A trumpet is not used by a timid person. And it certainly was not a timid person who used a voice sounding like a trumpet here, as we'll see in the rest of the chapter. John's attention is forcefully grabbed as he is told to write the things that he would see on a scroll and send the message to the seven churches listed in verse 11. In his fright, John turns around to see the one who speaks to him, only to see something else.

JESUS AND HIS CHURCH

1:12, Then I turned to see the voice that was speaking with me. And after turning, I saw seven golden lampstands. 13, And in the middle of the lampstands, I saw one like a son of man, clothed in a robe reaching to the feet and wrapped around the chest with a golden sash. 14, His head and His hair were white like white wool, like snow, and his eyes were like a flame of fire. 15, His feet were like burnished bronze when it has been heated to a glow in a furnace, and His voice was like the sound of many waters. 16, In His right hand He held seven stars, and out of his mouth came a sharp two-edged sword; and His face was like the sun shining in its strength.

The first thing John reports seeing is seven golden lampstands. The image I get is of lampstands on the ground but reaching chest-high on an average-sized person. We are told in verse 20 that each lampstand represents one of the seven churches to which John is writing. The characteristics of the lampstands are that they give light, are costly, and are autonomous. The purpose of each church is to give light to those living in their vicinity. God considers each church as unbelievably valuable. They each stand on their own or fall on their own. These lampstands are different from the lampstand of Israel, which was one lampstand with seven candles in one unit. In that case, the churches would not be autonomous, and the failure of one would affect the success of another. Praise the Lord for congregational autonomy!

Then John saw "one like a son of man" walking among the lampstands. After reading Revelation 1:12-16, you really must read Daniel 7:9 - 14. This is wonderful! Notice the similarities between the son of man in Revelation and the Ancient of Days in Daniel.

Table 3: Son of Man and Ancient of Days

Son of Man (Revelation)	Ancient of Days (Daniel)
Robe to his feet	Clothing white like snow
Golden sash	
Hair white like wool/snow	Hair white like wool
Eyes like blazing fire	Throne blazing like fire
Feet glowing like hot bronze	
A voice like rushing waters	
Face like the sun	

Notice that the Son of Man of Daniel is coming with the clouds of heaven. This reminds us of how Jesus ascended into heaven and how He is expected to return, as described in Acts 1:9-11. The unity of God's word is amazing!

Now, back to our passage. Where is Jesus? He is walking among the lampstands. He is with the churches. Remember that in His great commission, as recorded in Matthew 28:20, he said, "Surely I am with you always, to the very end of the age." He's keeping his promise!

Consider the attributes of the Son of Man. He is wearing a full-length robe with a golden sash, a clear reference to the high priesthood. Jesus is the great high priest who, by his own death, has made atonement for all sin for all time. And He only had to die once because He always lives to make intercession for us who have come in contact with his blood, by grace through faith, completed in our submission to Him through baptism.[XXVI]

Jesus' hair was white like wool, as white as snow, just like the ancient days of Daniel 7:9. He is ageless. He displays sovereign glory. He is magnificent! And his eyes of blazing fire only add to the aura. There is nothing hidden from his eyes. He knows all. He, therefore, has perfect judgment.

His eyes are bright and blazing as with fire, and his face glows, shining like the sun. This is the magnificent glory of the almighty! Remember how Moses' face glowed after spending time in the presence of God (Exodus 34:29). In Moses' case, he put a veil over his face so that people would not see his face glow because the glow would diminish over time (2 Corinthians 3:13-18). But in Christ, the veil is taken away. There is no end to the glow on Jesus' face because He is God. When one turns to Him, the veil over our hearts is removed, and we are transformed into His likeness in His presence.

He's holding seven stars in His right hand. Are these gold stars that you stick on your child's drawing? Or are they pointed plastic balls made to look like stars that we attach to our ceilings? Or are they real stars like you see in the night sky? How do they fit in His hand? How does this make sense at all? Is this an optical illusion? Is Jesus that powerful that He can hold seven suns in one hand while walking among seven lampstands and speaking to John? This is amazing beyond comprehension. But we are told in verse 20 that the stars are the messengers or angels of the seven churches. Jesus is showing his caring protection for the churches by holding their messengers in his own hand. Why are the messengers of the churches described as stars? A star is bright, it's hot, and it's powerful. Imagine having such a messenger of the church you attend being held in the right hand of Jesus. What does that say to you about Jesus' view of your congregation? Does that change how you feel about your congregation and your commitment toward it? Think about what these things mean. Feel Jesus' commitment to the church. Is that the kind of commitment you have to the church?

Look at his feet! How could you miss them? (Unless you can't take your eyes off that sword coming out of his mouth.) They're bright, like bronze glowing in a furnace. Get on the internet and do a search for "bronze glowing in a furnace" to get an idea of what this must have looked like. Bright, hot, incredible, powerful. Brass is moldable, harder than iron, and far more corrosion-resistant.[XXVII] I get the picture of enduring power. Think of how Daniel's vision of Rome was of feet mixed of iron and clay – brittle, breakable, temporary. Jesus' feet are strong, enduring, unbreakable. He can save truly! The pax-Romana was fake; the peace that comes through Christ is real, solid, and enduring.

What must it have looked like to see a double-edged sword protruding from his mouth? This visually represents Hebrews 4:12, *For the word of God is alive and active. Sharper than any double-edged sword, it penetrates even to dividing soul and spirit, joints and marrow; it judges the thoughts and attitudes of the heart.* It is my job to allow that double-edged sword to pierce my soul and spirit, to judge the thoughts and attitudes of my heart so they may be corrected, trained in righteousness, and that I might shine as a light to the world, attracting those I encounter to Christ.

Hold your hands over your ears! Jesus is about to speak. His voice is like the roar of many waters. What must that have sounded like? Get on the internet again and find a video for "Real Sound of Niagara Falls."[XXVIII] Oh, make sure you have the volume all the way up! Maybe that will give us some idea of what Jesus' voice sounded like. Consider the power, the depth, the continuity of his voice and how it must have shaken John. There is authority in this voice. When you hear this voice, no argument and no excuse will stand. The only response I have is to fall at his feet as though dead as John did.

JESUS AND JOHN

1:17 When I saw Him, I fell at His feet like a dead man. And He placed His right hand on me, saying, "Do not be afraid; I am the first and the last. 18, And the living One; and I was dead, and behold, I am alive forevermore, and I have the keys of death and of Hades. 19, Therefore, write the things which you have seen, and the things which are, and the things which will take place after these things. 20, As for the mystery of the seven stars which you saw in My right hand, and the seven golden lampstands: the seven stars are the angels of the seven churches, and the seven lampstands are the seven churches.

It is amazing what happens next! Here, John is lying at Jesus' feet as though dead, and Jesus places his right hand on John! Wait, didn't we just say there were seven stars in his right hand? What happened to them? As Dan Winkler said, *'Earlier, "seven stars," representing the leadership, personality, or messengers of seven congregations, were in his right hand. But, here, he has placed the seven stars aside to give his undivided attention to just one disciple, John! Thankfully, God is a God of the individual.*[9] God has such care for the individual. This is one of my favorite thoughts about God. Think about when Hagar fled away from Sarai's harsh treatment (Genesis 16). She was lost and alone and without food and water in the desert. God, my God, appeared to her, gave her what she needed, and promised to be with her. Hagar said, "You are the God who sees me." How wonderful that is. Let us be like that to those around us who need God's tender touch.

Notice that Jesus informs John that he has the keys to death and Hades. He, the living One, who died but is alive forevermore, has control of death and Hades. He's also the one who is the God of the individual. He's the one who wants all people to be saved and come to a knowledge of the truth. He's the one who is not willing that any should perish but that all should come to repentance. This includes you and me. Jesus can help us escape death and Hades and live eternally with him. Let's not miss his offer.

A WONDERFUL SAVIOR

With such a glorious savior, do we have anything to fear? The message is vital to Christians in every generation because it answers the question of whether being a Christian is worth it when the wicked can prosper and grow in power. This chapter contains at least 25 descriptions of our wonderful God and Savior. See the list below.

Table 4: A Wonderful Savior

Vs. 4: God, who is, who was, and who is to come.
Vs. 4: The Holy Spirit, complete in glory.
Vs. 5: Jesus, the faithful witness.
Vs. 5: Jesus, the firstborn from the dead, never to die again.
Vs. 5: Jesus, the ruler of the kings of the earth.
Vs. 5: Jesus, who loves us!
Vs. 5: Jesus, who freed us from our sins by his blood.
Vs. 6: Jesus, who made us kings and priests.
Vs. 6: God, to whom be glory and power forever and ever. Amen!
Vs. 7: Jesus, who will punish the wicked.
Vs. 8: Jesus, the Alpha and Omega.
Vs. 8: Jesus, who was and is and will always be.
Vs. 8: Jesus, who is the Almighty.
Vs. 13: Jesus, the Great High Priest.
Vs. 14: Jesus' head and hair depict the ageless sovereign glory of God.
Vs. 14: Jesus' eyes indicate the omniscient judge who can't be fooled.
Vs. 15: Jesus' feet of strength to save and offer hope to the persecuted believers.
Vs. 15: Jesus' voice of ultimate authority.
Vs. 16: Jesus' right hand of protection and caring.
Vs. 16: Jesus' mouth speaks the powerful message of hope.
Vs. 16: Jesus' face shining in all the magnificent glory of the Almighty.
Vs. 17: Jesus, the first and the last.
Vs. 18: Jesus, the Living One.
Vs. 18: Jesus, the one who was dead but is alive forever and ever!
Vs. 18: Jesus, the one who has power over death and the grave.

CHAPTER 4

A CHURCH UNDER PRESSURE

Revelation 2:1 to 3:22

I just spent the last chapter trying to help you understand that Revelation must be felt more than thought, and we will certainly get back to that. But now that we transition to the direct messages to each of the seven churches, there is much to be learned here from thinking more than feeling. Chapters 2 and 3 of Revelation focus on the condition of each congregation with a message often tailored to their geographical uniqueness. These two chapters have patterns, themes, and pictures typical of visions. These aspects are used to convey a message to our emotions to motivate correct behavior.

We will follow the similarities highlighted in the table below to simplify our approach to these messages. At the end of this chapter, I have included a list of most of the terms used in Revelation chapters 2 and 3 with a short definition. I hope you find it useful.

Table 5: Comparison of the Churches

Church Name	Ephesus	Smyrna	Pergamum	Thyatira *	Sardis *	Philadelphia *	Laodicea *
Salutation	2:1a: To the angel of the church in Ephesus write:	2:8a: To the angel of the church in Smyrna write:	2:12a: To the angel of the church in Pergamum write:	2:18a: To the angel of the church in Thyatira write:	3:1a: To the angel of the church in Sardis write:	3:7a: To the angel of the church in Philadelphia write:	3:14a: To the angel of the church in Laodicea write:
Jesus' Description	2:1b: The One who holds the seven stars in His right hand, the One who walks among the seven golden lampstands	2:8b: The first and the last, who was dead, and has come to life.	2:12b: The One who has the sharp two-edged sword.	2:18b: The Son of God, who has eyes like a flame of fire, and feet like burnished bronze.	3:1b: He who has the seven spirits of God and the seven stars.	3:7b: He who is holy, who is true, who has the key of David, who opens and no one will shut, and who shuts and no one opens.	3:14b: The Amen, the faithful and true Witness, the Origin of the creation of God
I know!	2:2: I know your deeds	2:9: I know your tribulation	2:13: I know where you dwell	2:19: I know your deeds	3:1c: I know your deeds	3:8: I know your deeds.	3:15: I know your deeds
Commendation	2:2-3	2:09	2:13	2:19		3:8-10	
Correction	2:04		2:14-15	2:20-21	3:1c-2		3:15-18
Commands	2:05	2:10	2:16	2:22-23	3:03	3:11	3:19-20
Commendation	2:06			2:24-25	3:04		
Command to Listen!	2:7a: The one who has an ear, let him hear what the Spirit says to the churches.	2:11a: The one who has an ear, let him hear what the Spirit says to the churches.	2:17a: The one who has an ear, let him hear what the Spirit says to the churches.	2:29: The one who has an ear, let him hear what the Spirit says to the churches.	3:6: The one who has an ear, let him hear what the Spirit says to the churches.	3:13: The one who has an ear, let him hear what the Spirit says to the churches.	3:22: The one who has an ear, let him hear what the Spirit says to the churches.
Promise to overcomers	2:7b	2:11b	2:17b	2:26-28	3:05	3:12	3:21

* The order of the admonition to Listen! and the Promise to Overcomers is reversed for these churches.

PATTERN

Notice that there is one column for each of the seven churches and one row for each of the nine steps in the pattern of the letters. We'll discuss this pattern shortly. The solid bar between Thyatira and Sardis indicates that the first 4 churches are in chapter 2, while the last 3 are in chapter 3. The first four seem to emphasize the doctrinal purity of the churches, while the last three seem to emphasize the spiritual devotion of the churches. Many of the groups of seven in Revelation are split into two groups. Typically, the first is a group of four, and the second is three. However, this pattern is not followed for the order of the admonition to Listen and the Promise to Overcomers – the first three churches are given the admonition to listen before the promise to overcomers. The last four churches have the promise to overcomers given before the admonition to listen.

As you can see, the letters have a very noticeable pattern. Each letter starts with the salutation to whom the letter is written, followed by a description of Jesus and a statement of what Jesus knows about the church being addressed. In all but two cases, Jesus has something commendable to say about them, and then in all but two cases, Jesus has some correction to offer the church. Each church then receives commands with promises and warnings. Three churches then receive a commendation that appears in a "there is SOME good in you" manner. Finally, each letter ends with the command to listen and the promise to overcomers.

Each letter starts the same way, "To the angel of the church in [*city name*], write." The literal translation for the word "angel" is "messenger". Remember, we noticed that the stars in Jesus' right hand are the angels of the seven churches. Jesus, who is holding the seven stars, is telling John to write a letter to each of the seven stars in his hand! Aren't God's methods amazing? It is God's way always to send people to minister to people.

THE DESCRIPTION OF JESUS AND HIS MESSAGE

One of the great patterns of these letters is that at the start of each letter, there is a description of Jesus, with a hint given as to what the message of that church involves.

EPHESUS Revelation 2:1-7

In the description of Jesus in the letter to Ephesus (2:1), he is shown holding the seven stars and walking among the seven golden lampstands. Previously, we noticed that the stars were the angels of the seven churches, and the lampstands were the seven churches. Jesus' message to the Ephesians (2:5) is that he will remove their lampstand if they do not repent.

SMYRNA Revelation 2:8-11

Jesus' message to the church at Smyrna (2:8,10b) is this: "I died and came to life again because I am the first and the last, and I have an eternal commitment." He calls the people of Smyrna to have a lifetime commitment even if they are called to suffer to death because he gives them the promise of a resurrection like his.

PERGAMUM Revelation 2:12-17

The message to Pergamum highlights the sharp two-edged sword (2:12,16-17). In verse 16 of both chapters 1 and 2, we see the two-edged sword coming out of Jesus' mouth! As we stated before, this is a visual representation of Hebrews 4:12. The two-edged sword is the word of God. Through His word, those who hold to the teaching of Balaam and the teaching of the Nicolaitans will be judged, and those who are faithful will be justified. Jesus' words are our judge, as we see in John 12:48.

THYATIRA Revelation 2:18-29

To Thyatira, Jesus has eyes like blazing fire and feet like burnished bronze (2:18, 23, 26-28). Again, these are things we saw in the description of Jesus in Revelation 1:14,15. He searches our minds and hearts with his eyes like blazing fire or flames of fire. Nothing is hidden from the sight of such eyes! As feet like burnished bronze represent unbreakable authority, Jesus will give authority to rule to those who keep his works – notice the action phrase, "keep his works" – till the end. Where Jesus' blazing fiery eyes are highlighted, he gives the morning star to those who overcome.

SARDIS Revelation 3:1-6

Jesus has the seven spirits of God and the seven stars in his message to Sardis (3:1, 4-5). The seven spirits represent the totality of wisdom and insight, and the seven stars are the messengers of the seven churches. He has wisdom and insight to help the faithful.

PHILADELPHIA Revelation 3:7-13

In the case of Philadelphia, we see Jesus holding the key of David (3:7-13). Jesus is the holy one, the true one, and no one can shut the doors that he has opened. What he has shut, no one can open. To the Jews, who thought they belonged to David but who persecuted the Christians, the door was shut. But to the penitent believers, the door to the temple of heaven is open and they who conquer may enter.

LAODICEA Revelation 3:14-22

Finally, to Laodicea (3:14-22), Jesus is the Amen, the faithful and true witness, the ruler of God's creation. He calls Laodicea to the faithful and true witness that they had left. Overcomers would get to share in the rule of Christ.

LISTEN!

Every message concludes with the command to listen! "He who has an ear to hear, let him hear what the Spirit says to the churches." Here, the Spirit of God is talking directly to the churches. Each letter is directed to one church but is meant for all. The message is not meant for the Elders, Ministers, or the so-called Ecclesiastical leaders but for the people of the churches.

Men do not receive spiritual information regarding their salvation from any inner impulses, dreams, impressions, or inner strivings of the soul but by listening to the words given by the Holy Spirit and written down for us. 'This shows that God's revelations are spoken to man, not put into his heart through some mysterious spiritual power.' [XXIX]

OVERCOMER'S PROMISE

In each message, there is a promise to those who conquer or overcome their trials. We saw in a previous section that Jesus's description matched his message. Here, too, the promise to overcome also matches Jesus' description and the message to that church.

EPHESUS Revelation 2:1-7

Jesus holds the essence of the churches in his hands and walks among them, giving them his support. He has a great interest in the strength and survival of the churches. His message to Ephesus is about their deeds, labor, and perseverance. They have done many things well, even avoiding the influence of people who are false in their claims. They have shown the ability to judge the deeds of false brothers, but they have left their love for Jesus – their first love. All their excellent work has become a matter of their own works of godliness looking good to others, not of devotion and love for their Lord. It is good to hate the deeds of the Nicolaitans, but not from a self-righteous perspective. Jesus, being the one who walks among the churches for their health and strength, promises eternal life to those who overcome because they will be allowed to eat of the Tree of Life. God would have us hate the deeds of the erring but not the person who is erring. Consider the fact that all the letters of the New Testament were written to churches that were erring in some manner. No lack of love is felt in those letters – even to Galatia and Corinth, who had severe issues. But Ephesus had crossed that line in their view of the erring.

SMYRNA Revelation 2:8-11

Jesus is the first and the last. He died and has come to life. His message to Smyrna is that they will suffer many things. Many will die. But Jesus has overcome death, so the second death will not hurt anyone who overcomes the temptation to give up. For those who are faithful to Jesus till death there will be no second death. The second death is the condemnation of eternal separation from the giver of life. Stay faithful till the end, experience the eternal gift of life by being in the presence of the giver of life, and, along with the Ephesians, enjoy eating the tree of life.

PERGAMUM Revelation 2:12-17

To Pergamum, Jesus is the one with the sharp double-edged sword. In Jesus' message to Pergamum,[xxx] we see the sword coming out of his mouth, just as we did in the description of Jesus.[xxxi] We know that the sword is the word of God, which is also the word by which we are judged or acquitted. The people of Pergamum had the misfortune of living where Satan had his throne – that is, this was the center of Roman rule in the area, the center of Roman emperor worship, and the center of much idol worship. For example, the temple to Zeus had a 40' high altar. Rome ruled by the sword, which is why Jesus is shown ruling here with a much more powerful sword than that of Rome. The overcomers here are represented as the ones who got to eat the "hidden" manna. The hidden manna is a reference to Christ. It is hidden because those not in Christ cannot see it or understand it. As we meditate on the words of our Lord, are we not partaking of the hidden manna? As we partake in the Lord's supper each week, are we not partaking of the hidden manna? But these are only appetizers for the hidden manna we will enjoy in heaven. The white stone we receive at our baptism is our ticket into heaven to get to enjoy that eternally sustaining hidden manna. The stone is white because it represents holiness, and the name on it is only known to the one who receives it, but certainly it says, "The image of Christ"!

THYATIRA Revelation 2:18-29

The description of Jesus to Thyatira harkens back to the description of Jesus in chapter 1, verses 14-15. His eyes are like blazing fire – there is nothing he doesn't see. He sees right through every concealed thing to its essence. There were those in Thyatira who had fallen into the false worship of idols, as Jezebel had led Ahab and Israel into the same.[XXXII] Those who refused to repent would be cast on a bed of suffering, so all the churches would know that Jesus' eyes see everything – he searches hearts and minds – nothing is hidden from his eyes.

Like burnished bronze, his feet are strong, enduring, unbreakable, powerful, and full of authority. There is no Achilles' heel. There is no vulnerability. Those who held fast to righteousness would be given authority over the nations. Remember how Jesus gave authority to his disciples when he sent them out to preach,[XXXIII] so now he gives authority over the nations to the overcomers. Hold fast to what you have until Jesus comes so that you will rule over the nations with an iron rod. That is an amazing promise. The overcomer receives authority from Jesus just as Jesus received it from his Father. He will also receive the Morning Star. Peter speaks of the morning star rising in your hearts,[XXXIV] and John[XXXV] identifies Jesus as the morning star. Receiving the morning star and having it rise in your heart refers to Christ in you, the hope of glory![XXXVI]

SARDIS Revelation 3:1-6

As to Ephesus, Jesus had seven stars and walked among the seven golden lampstands. To Sardis, he had seven spirits of God and seven stars. The number seven here represents completeness. The spirits and the stars represent life. Many people in the church at Sardis had not completed their work. They fell asleep on the job! They had been going strong with energy and "hit a wall," "gave up the ghost," and "died on the vine." They had been a sign of the glory of God but took their eyes off of Jesus and got tired out. They are called to open their eyes, look at the one who is with the seven spirits and holds the seven stars, and be revived. Those who do so will be redeemed and purified as they are dressed in white and have their names permanently printed in the Book of Life so that Jesus acknowledges them before God.

PHILADELPHIA Revelation 3:7-13

To Philadelphia, Jesus is the holy and true holder of the keys of David. What he opens or shuts is in that position, regardless of who tries to change it. The letter to Philadelphia is surprisingly long for a church for which Jesus has no reprimand. Jesus has opened a door for them, and through much trial, they have been faithful amid many who claim to be godly but aren't. Consider carefully the church you are a part of. Are you among people who claim to be godly but are not because the church is not the church of Christ? Christ came to build His church. Putting another name on it means it's someone else's church. Many claim to be Christians but are of the church of Satan. Will God make them come and bow down to the faithful church to make them know that He has loved the church of Christ, His church? But we must do as Jesus admonished Philadelphia, "Hold firmly to what you have so that no one will take your crown." The key of David is about who the Lord's possession is. So, the one who overcomes has a permanent place as a pillar in the temple of God. He is identified as God's possession. He has a glorious place in God's city, the new Jerusalem. Let us hold firmly to what we have!

LAODICEA Revelation 3:14-22

Jesus is represented as three ideas to Laodicea. The Amen (so shall it be; the end), the faithful and true witness (the now), and the Origin of the creation of God (the beginning). Jesus tells the people of Laodicea that they do not know their own condition. They think they are faithful to God, but they are just lukewarm people, going through the physical motions without heart. God is looking for the application of the heart and soul to what we do and to a heart change. Jesus wants them to make a true decision, "Be completely devoted to me from the heart or be completely opposed to me from the heart. But if you persist in having one foot in the world and one foot in the church, I'll decide for you, which will be painful for both of us."

"Here I am! I stand at the door and knock. If anyone hears my voice and opens the door, I will come in and eat with that person, and they, with me."[XXXVII] It is one of the most misused verses in all of scripture. The people that Jesus is speaking to are Christians – they are currently in His church. He stands at their door and knocks. He invites them to open the door and rejoin him in complete and full-hearted fellowship. This is not an invitation to the lost simply to welcome him into their hearts and be saved. That would oppose what Jesus said in Matthew 28:18-20, Mark 16:15-16 and John 3:5. Jesus cannot contradict himself.

Jesus was faithful through all the trials he faced on earth and was victorious in winning the battle against Satan's many attacks so that we might have the opportunity of eternal salvation. If we are victorious, he, the faithful and true witness, will allow us to sit with him on his throne just as he sits with the Father on His throne. How wonderful and amazing is that?

DOCTRINAL PURITY

As we noted before, there are letters to four churches in chapter 2 of Revelation and three in chapter 3, which follow a common grouping of the sevens in the book. It also appears that in the first four cities, there is a progression of the difference in their doctrinal purity. However, this common grouping reverses in that the first three letters have the command to listen preceding the promise to overcomers. The last four letters have the command to listen after the promise to overcomers. Perhaps this is to emphasize the universal nature of the message, along with the universal nature of the command to listen, "Whoever has ears to hear, let him hear what the Spirit says to the churches." Although each letter is specific to the church it addresses, the message must be heard and applied to each church and every member.

Let's look at the four churches of Revelation 2 and their doctrinal purity. It is important to note that the term "deeds" is short for "doctrinal soundness" in these letters. Where the word "deeds" is used, you can also think of "doctrinal soundness."

EPHESUS Revelation 2:1-7

'I know your deeds and your labor and perseverance, and that you cannot tolerate evil people, and you have put those who call themselves apostles to the test, and they are not, and you found them to be false.'[XXXVIII]

SMYRNA Revelation 2:8-11

'I know your tribulation and your poverty (but you are rich), and the slander by those who say they are Jews and are not, but are a synagogue of Satan.'[XXXIX]

PERGAMUM Revelation 2:12-17

'But I have a few things against you because you have some there who hold the teaching of Balaam, who kept teaching Balak to put an obstacle before the sons of Israel, to eat things sacrificed to idols, and to commit sexual immorality. So, you, too, have some who, in the same way, hold to the teaching of the Nicolaitans.'[XL]

THYATIRA Revelation 2:18-29

'But I have this against you, that you tolerate the woman Jezebel, who calls herself a prophetess, and she teaches and leads My bondservants astray so that they commit sexual immorality and eat things sacrificed to idols.'[XLI]

Do you see the progression from being overly strict doctrinally to having no concern about doctrinal purity? Ephesus would not tolerate the Nicolaitans, but they left their first love in their overemphasis on doctrinal purity. They loved doctrinal purity more than their love for the Lord. This sounds a lot like Jesus's argument with the Pharisees, who complained about his healing on the Sabbath. Jesus' answer was that if they had understood what God meant when he said, "I desire compassion, rather than sacrifice," they would not have condemned the innocent. [XLII] Jesus had no correction for Smyrna, but Pergamum had tolerated false doctrine, and Thyatira had downright accepted a false prophet who taught people to commit sexual immorality and eat things sacrificed to idols.

SPIRITUAL SOUNDNESS

As we look through the letters to the churches in Revelation chapter 3, we see a progression in spirituality.

SARDIS Revelation 3:1-6

'I know your deeds, that you have a name, that you are alive, and yet you are dead.'[XLIII]

PHILADELPHIA Revelation 3:7-13

'I know your deeds. Behold, I have put before you an open door which no one can shut because you have a little power, and have followed My word, and have not denied My name.'[XLIV]

LAODICEA Revelation 3:14-22

'I know your deeds, that you are neither cold nor hot; I wish that you were cold or hot. So, because you are lukewarm and neither hot nor cold, I will vomit you out of My mouth.'[XLV]

Sardis is putting on a show of spirituality, but they are dead. Philadelphia is alive and genuine in its spirituality. Laodicea has fallen into complacency. All three appear to be maintaining doctrinal purity.

CONCLUSION

It is possible to have deeds or be doctrinally sound without spirituality, as Ephesus did. Still, it is impossible to have true spirituality without deeds and doctrinal soundness, as in the case of Sardis. Notice the similarity of the description of Jesus in the letters to Ephesus and Sardis. Both had deeds but were dead spiritually. Sardis was not following through on their deeds because they were dead spiritually. Ephesus was dead spiritually because they gave too much credence to correct deeds. Having complete and correct deeds is necessary, but it must be led by spirituality, not become so important to the exclusion of spirituality. The view held by Ephesus leads a church to lose its love for the erring and even to fail to maintain fellowship with those who desire to allow deeds to grow out of spirituality.

With these very hard-hitting letters, Jesus is working to bring the churches in line and prepare them for the persecution they will continue to face so that they will faithfully endure.

Table 6: Terms and Definitions

Terms used in Revelation chapters 2 and 3.

2:1 **Angel** – Messenger of the church / the church's real nature and inner state.

2:1 **holds the seven stars in his right hand**

- Jesus holds the life and death of each church in his hands.
- Isaiah 41:10 ...I will uphold you with my righteous right hand.

2:1 **Walks among the seven golden lampstands**

They give light.
- Golden – costly.
- They are autonomous, unlike the lampstand of Israel, which is one stand with seven candles.
- Jesus walked among them. He was with them. Matthew 28:20: What a comfort!

2:6 **Nicolaitans** – They participated in the orgies of the pagan religions of the area. Their doctrines appear to have been similar to those of Balaam and Jezebel.

2:7 **Tree of Life**

- Reference to Genesis 3:22, from which Adam and Eve were banished.
- Stands for spiritual sustenance, the food of righteousness.[XLVI]
- Christ[XLVII]

2:7 **Paradise of God**

- Reference to the Genesis paradise
- This is the real and eternal paradise – Heaven.

2:9, 3:9 **False Jews** – Jews by birth who had not become Christians.

2:9, 3:9 **Synagogue of Satan** – Jews who fought against Christ and persecuted Christians.

2:10 **Ten Days** – a complete period

2:10 **Crown of Life** – Life after death. Smyrna was the "crown" of emperor worship, which offered no hope after death.

2:11 **Second death** – Hell

2:12 **Sharp, double-edged sword** – The word of God[XLVIII]

2:13 **Where Satan lives/has his throne** – Seat of emperor worship.

2:13 **Antipas, my faithful witness** – A person or people who were martyred for their faith.

2:16 **Sword of my mouth** – The word of God

2:17 **Hidden manna** – Jesus

2:17 **White stone** – a stone given to someone acquitted of a crime, a freed slave, the winner of a race, a victorious winner.

2:17 **New name known only to the recipient**.

- New name – new status/relationship.
- A new name is given when our situation changes.
- It is unique to the recipient.

2:18 **Eyes like burning fire** – He misses nothing. Nothing is hidden from his sight.[XLIX]

2:18 **Feet like burnished bronze** – Destructive power.

2:20 **Jezebel the prophetess** – a church member who was teaching falsehood and was allowed to do so.

2:22 **Bed of suffering** – Jezebel would be cast from the bed of fornication into the bed of suffering.

2:24 **Satan's deep secrets** – Lies of Satan.

2:26 **Authority over the nations** – Contrary to appearances, Jesus already has this (vs. 27).

2:28 **Morning star** – Christ

3:1 **Seven spirits of God**

- The Holy Spirit
- The full spirit of God.
- Seven names of the Spirit[L]
    o The Spirit of the Lord
    o The Spirit of Wisdom
    o The Spirit of Understanding
    o The Spirit of Counsel
    o The Spirit of Strength
    o The Spirit of Knowledge
    o The Spirit of the Fear of the Lord

3:4-5, 18 **Dressed in white** – Those who are justified, pure and holy.

3:5 **Book of Life** – The record of the saved.

3:7 **Key of David**

- A clear reference to Christ, who was promised to be the son of David.
- Undisputed authority to admit or exclude people from heaven.

CHAPTER 5

THE THRONE OF GOD

Revelation 4:1 to 5:14

The message of Revelation is meant to be felt more than thought. It is meant to be visualized and experienced, not picked through like a scientific document or training manual. Have you ever noticed that sometimes the sun seems much brighter as the storm clouds gather to cover the sun? When a commander prepares his troops for the battle, he does his best to sound courageous and powerful and project the message that victory is assured. It is like the bright light before a storm. If you're a *Lord of the Rings* fan, there is a great example of this before the last battle in *The Return of the King* movie. This is what we see in chapters 4 and 5 of Revelation. The bright light before the storm. The encouragement before the battle. In John 14:1, Jesus' words are recorded as follows, "Do not let your hearts be troubled. Trust in God; trust also in me." Stick with your commanding officer, Jesus, and victory is assured!

THE OPEN DOOR

4:1, After this, I looked, and there before me was a door standing open in heaven. And the voice I had first heard speaking to me like a trumpet said, "Come up here, and I will show you what must take place after this." 2, At once, I was in the Spirit, and there before me was a throne in heaven with someone sitting on it.

It was Sunday, the Lord's Day. John was worshiping in the Spirit and saw a vision of the Lord, who gave him a commission and seven letters, one to each of the seven churches, but all the letters were also to all the churches. After this, John looks up and sees an open door in heaven. This is another amazing thing to consider. Spiritually, we can see into heaven, and the door is open for us to enter. As Christians, we live there already, even as we live here on earth. Consider Colossians 3:1-4: *Since then, you have been raised with Christ, set your hearts on things above, where Christ is, seated at the right hand of God. Set your minds on things above, not on earthly things. For you died, and your life is now hidden with Christ in God. When Christ, who is your life, appears, then you also will appear with him in glory.* Ephesians 2:6 *And God raised us up with Christ and seated us with him in the heavenly realms in Christ Jesus.* Philippians 3:20 *But our citizenship is in heaven. And we eagerly await a Savior from there, the Lord Jesus Christ.* The open door to heaven should be a great encouragement to us. We have the assurance of the eternal rest promised to those who are faithful till the end.

John hears Jesus' voice calling him up to heaven, where he will be shown what must take place "after this." After what? Simply after that moment in time for John. There is no time frame given here for how soon these things would occur, but they were after John received the letters he was to send. Suddenly, he appeared in heaven, in the Spirit. John was already in the Spirit in his worship, but now he is taken to heaven in the Spirit, probably meaning that he was not physically taken there but through a vision.

THE THRONE SCENE

4:2, *There before me was a throne in heaven with someone sitting on it. 3 And the one who sat there had the appearance of a jasper and ruby. A rainbow that shone like an emerald encircled the throne. 4, Surrounding the throne were twenty-four other thrones, and seated on them were twenty-four elders. They were dressed in white and had crowns of gold on their heads. 5, From the throne came flashes of lightning, rumblings, and peals of thunder. In front of the throne, seven lamps were blazing. These are the seven spirits of God. 6, Also, in front of the throne, there was what looked like a sea of glass, clear as crystal. In the center, around the throne, were four living creatures, and they were covered with eyes, in front, and in back. 7, The first living creature was like a lion, the second was like an ox, the third had a face like a man, and the fourth was like a flying eagle. 8, Each of the four living creatures had six wings and was covered with eyes all around, even under its wings.*

John sees before him a throne which is in heaven. In the Old Testament, God was enthroned on the ark between the two cherubim.[LI] He is enthroned in heaven,[LII] on high,[LIII] in Zion,[LIV] above the circle of the earth [LV], and among the hosts of heaven.[LVI] These are just a sampling of the descriptions of God's throne room. The idea of God's throne is more significant in Revelation than any other book in the Bible. No matter what we feel like we are going through, we must be aware of who is in control. Neither Rome, the United States, nor anyone else, no matter how powerful they may feel or seem to be at the moment, is in control. We have a God who knows His people and can rescue them from any trouble, even if that means taking them home to be with Him.

GOD ON HIS THRONE

Did you see the person on the throne? He has the appearance of jasper and ruby. Jasper is a crystal that is typically multicolored. Ruby is an exceptionally beautiful, blood-red-colored stone. Doesn't this seem to be a reference to Joseph's coat of many colors that his brothers dipped in blood when they sold him into slavery? God sent Joseph to Egypt through his brothers' sin to save the world from starvation in the coming famine. In the same way, Jesus shed his own blood as he died on the cross to save people of many colors. Wonderful!

Jasper and ruby are precious gems, but the jasper stone is found almost everywhere in the world. God is the most precious entity in existence, but He is everywhere like Jasper, and His presence is beautiful like the ruby. This amazing person is surrounded by a rainbow that looks like an emerald. The emerald crystal is a beautiful stone that has a green color but can be cut in such a way as to produce a most beautiful rainbow with very distinct and bright rainbow colors. The emerald is a classic color that can symbolize refinement, wealth, and royalty. [LVII] The rainbow symbolizes a merciful, covenant-keeping God whose ultimate goal is not to destroy His creation but to save it. [LVIII]

THE 24 THRONES

Now, we are told of 24 other thrones that surround the throne of God. I imagine that these thrones are in a circle around God's throne with an opening to the front of God's throne to make room for the sea of glass, but the 24 elders are facing God, whom they constantly worship.

Who are these 24 elders? How are they dressed? They are dressed in white and have crowns of gold on their heads. Of course, white is for purity. In the letter to Sardis, [LIX] we saw that those who do not soil their clothes by sin are dressed in white. Those who are victorious because of God's precious and providential care will also be dressed in white. From Revelation 7:14, we understand that one gets a white robe by washing it clean in the blood of the Lamb. Isn't this an obvious reference to our baptism? The 24 elders also had crowns of gold, signifying wealth and the right to rule. In the letter to Thyatira, Jesus promises that those who are victorious will be given authority over the nations and will rule over them, [LX] so they are reigning with God and have authority over the nations. And I bet that their crowns were engraved with the words "Holiness to the Lord." [LXI] The number 12 represents the people of God, and so the 24 elders may be the 12 tribes and the 12 apostles. Another view is that there are 12 apostles, who were all Jews, and 12 Gentiles, who are unnamed. Whatever the case, it is the church. It is God's kingdom.

BEFORE THE THRONE

Within the circle of the 24 elders, there is a smaller circle around God's throne with a gap in front of the throne for the seven lamps. This is the circle of the four living creatures. In front of God's throne, in the space allowed by the gap between two of the four creatures, are seven lamps blazing which are the seven spirits or the sevenfold Spirit of God. This is the complete spirit of God. Remember that we saw seven candlesticks on earth that represented the seven churches. Here, we see seven lamps, which are the seven spirits. Both have a flame. Does not the flame in the candlesticks represent the spirit of God that is living in the church? Does that not make the admonition of 1 Thessalonians 5:19, in the context of Christian conduct, even more powerful? "Quench not the Spirit!"

Then, in the gap between two of the 24 elders, in front of the throne, is the sea of glass, clear as crystal. It is a sea of glass. The water is calm, clear, and deep. There is no ripple. In many references to water in the Bible, water is a raging, scary thing, often representing the raging of the nations. But this water is calm and clear, reminding me of Psalm 23:2, where the Lord promises David to lead him beside quiet waters. Are these waters inviting me to drink and be refreshed with God's precious care? Or are they meant for separation, emphasizing God's holiness, the holiness of the four creatures, and the holiness of the 24 elders? In either case, or both cases, it is a fantastic sight. But if that isn't fantastic enough, there are flashes of lightning, rumbling, and peals of thunder emanating from the throne. Why is God represented in such an awesome and fearful way? As such an awesome sight to behold? God has the power to take care of me! Whatever my "light and momentary troubles"[LXII] are, God controls everything and can handle all enemies.

THE FOUR CREATURES

Now, let's look a little closer at the sight of the four living creatures. How amazing! Why is their living nature highlighted? Apparently, this is for us to be sure that they aren't just some parts of a vision but a real part of the throne room scene. We are directed to their plethora of eyes twice: verse 6 says that they were covered with eyes front and back, and verse 8 says they were covered with eyes all around, even under their wings. With these many eyes, they must be all-seeing. But this feeds into the way they never stop worshipping God as "Holy, Holy, Holy." They are endlessly looking out for God's reputation and character. Each living creature has six wings, just like the seraphim (fiery ones) that Isaiah saw, [LXIII] and their chant is remarkably similar. Ezekiel also described these creatures in his visions of the Lord [LXIV], but in Ezekiel 10, they are called cherubim. For Ezekiel, they are God's chariot, which speaks of judgment because they carry him to war. These living creatures are also represented in the ark of the covenant that God commanded and directed Moses to build. There also they are called cherubim.[LXV]

WORSHIP OF GOD

4:8, Each of the four living creatures had six wings and was covered with eyes all around, even under its wings. Day and night, they never stop saying:

"'Holy, holy, holy

is the Lord God Almighty,'

who was, and is, and is to come."

9, Whenever the living creatures give glory, honor, and thanks to Him who sits on the throne and who lives forever and ever. 10, the twenty-four elders fall down before Him who sits on the throne and worship Him, who lives forever and ever. They lay their crowns before the throne and say:

In the worship of God, we see many things in groups of three. God's attributes are most often described by groups of three words or phrases. The most stable formulation for the legs of a stool is three legs. That God is our strength is symbolized by how he is described. His identity is made known in three words, "Lord God Almighty." His nature in relation to all other beings is emphasized by being said three times, "Holy, holy, holy." Then, God's eternal nature is spoken through three phrases, "who was, and is, and is to come." It's as if saying that God is the one who was Holy in the past, who is Holy now, and who will be Holy in the future. Notice the worship of the living creatures; they give glory, honor, and thanks to God – three words. Then, the 24 elders, in their worship, say that God is worthy to receive glory, honor, and power, again three words.

Did you notice how the elders worship God? They fall down before God and lay their crowns before him, essentially saying, "These belong to you!" It is common in the Christian world to talk about people who do good works, gaining jewels on their crowns. My wife has many precious jewels on her crown for the many gracious and super-serving things she does, especially in being patient with me. If I were to have a crown, I like the thought of laying it down before God and giving it to Him. I want to give Him as big a crown as possible for His glory. The other fantastic thing about this scene is that the worship continues forever. Day and night, they never stop repeating this worship. This is not idle, rote worship. This is the worship of those who are amazed by the one who is before them.

THE SCROLL

5:1 Then I saw in the right hand of Him who sat on the throne a scroll with writing on both sides and sealed with seven seals. 2, And I saw a mighty angel proclaiming in a loud voice, "Who is worthy to break the seals and open the scroll?" 3, But no one in heaven or on earth or under the earth could open the scroll or even look inside it. 4, I wept and wept because no one was found who was worthy to open the scroll or look inside.

A scroll is in God's right hand, so this is an important book. Remember how Jesus held the seven stars in his right hand – the stars being the angels of the seven churches. Jesus touched John with his right hand. Now, God holds a scroll with his right hand. Things of importance are done with the right hand. This is why those of us who are left-handed are more spiritual – we reserve special things for the right hand. (Okay, I'm kidding). The scroll is unusual in that it has writing on both sides, but this indicates that it is the complete will of God. It is also exceedingly special because it is perfectly sealed, having seven seals.

Suddenly, the mighty angel appears with a mighty challenge. "Who is worthy to break the seals and open the scroll?" He's not shy about his challenge, either. This is proclaimed in a loud voice. A search is made in all of heaven and earth, and no one is found to be worthy. No one could open the scroll or even look inside it. This made John incredibly sad, and he wept bitterly. Why did this affect him so much? Why was it such an emotional event that no one was found worthy of opening the scroll? We aren't directly told, but the fact that John was so moved by this should indicate to us the importance of one who is worthy and able to open and read the scroll. What was so important or special about this scroll? As we will see in Revelation 6, these seals are about judgment. This scroll and its seals must only be opened by one who has the power to control the contents of the book. As we can see, that requires a lot of power.

THE LAMB

5:5, Then one of the elders said to me, "Do not weep! See, the Lion of the tribe of Judah, the Root of David, has triumphed. He is able to open the scroll and its seven seals." 6, Then I saw a Lamb, looking as if it had been slain, standing at the center of the throne, encircled by the four living creatures and the elders. The Lamb had seven horns and seven eyes, which are the seven spirits of God sent out into all the earth. 7, He went and took the scroll from the right hand of him who sat on the throne. 8, And when he had taken it, the four living creatures and the twenty-four elders fell down before the Lamb. Each one had a harp, and they were holding golden bowls full of incense, which are the prayers of God's people.

Finally, John is told by an elder not to weep. He is told, "Look, the Lion of the tribe of Judah is able to open the scroll and its seven seals." But John doesn't see a lion. He sees a lamb. And not just any lamb, but one who looks like it had been slain. But first, he is the Lion of the tribe of Judah. The lion is strength, courage, and power. He is royalty with wisdom and justice. He is protection. These things are not *for* Judah but *of* Judah and for the people of Christ. As in Isaiah 11:1,10, He is the Root of David. David, the man after God's own heart, was the quintessential member of the tribe of Judah, that is until Christ came into the world. So, Jesus is David's root. The unity and symmetry of scripture never cease to amaze me!

Never mind all that power and beauty. John actually sees a lamb that looks like it has been slaughtered. There is no beauty there. Imagine the bloody mess of matted wool. Wounds deep in the heart and feet. But this slaughtered lamb is standing; it's not dead at all. Not only that, but the lamb also has seven horns. If horns represent strength and seven represents completeness, then this lamb that had been slaughtered has complete strength. Of course it does! This is the one who gave himself up to be slaughtered, having the power to rise from the dead. And through whom did he rise from the dead? Well, through the Spirit. So, it makes sense that the lamb would have seven eyes, which, as we are told, are the seven spirits or sevenfold spirit of God – the complete spirit of God.

Did you notice where the lamb was standing? At the center of the throne. This is where God is. They are both surrounded by the four living creatures and, around them, the 24 elders. Before the throne[LXVI] are seven lamps blazing, and the lamb has seven eyes. Both are said to be the seven spirits of God. Here, we have God's throne surrounded by the 24 elders representing his people. Earlier[LXVII] on earth, we saw that Jesus was walking among the seven lampstands – the church. God's presence is with his people, the church! These people were going through great persecution and needed to know that God was right there with them! We need to know that God is right here with his church. His presence is still with His faithful people. Let's make sure that designation applies to us!

After the lamb took the scroll, the four living creatures and the 24 elders fell down before the lamb. These are the same beings that had been falling down and worshipping God on his throne day and night forever. Now, we see them falling down before the lamb. Only God is worshipped. The Lamb is God. These 28 beings each also had a harp and a golden bowl full of incense. We never see them do anything with the harps; they are never given meaning. However, we are told that the golden bowls full of incense symbolize the prayers of the saints. I can't wait till we get to Revelation 8, where we will see more about the prayers of God's people. In the meantime, consider the fact that the golden bowls full of incense are symbolic of something else, so the harps must be symbolic of something as well. Probably, they signify the voices of worship, which, as we see in verse 9, they are engaged in singing.

WORSHIP OF THE LAMB

From Revelation 5, verse 8 above, we know that the four living creatures and the 24 elders are singing the new song below.

THE 4 CREATURES AND 24 ELDERS

5:9 And they sang a new song, saying:

"You are worthy to take the scroll and to open its seals because you were slain, and with your blood, you purchased for God persons from every tribe and language and people and nation. 10, You have made them to be a kingdom and priests to serve our God, and they will reign on the earth."

In verse 5, we see that the lamb is worthy because he has triumphed like a lion. Now we see how he triumphed. He was slain, and through his blood, people from everywhere on earth were purchased for God. Notice how the people of the earth, of creation, are described: "from every tribe, language, people, nation. Four descriptions. Things of creation have four attributes. Things of God have three attributes. So, Jesus purchased people from everywhere for God by his blood. They are brought into his kingdom and made to be priests to serve God. Everyone in the church of Christ is a priest. There is no need or requirement for an earthly priesthood or clergy. Each person can go directly to God through Christ. The kingdom is present on earth now, and those whom Jesus has added to His church are members of that kingdom and are reigning now. As difficult as that is for us to believe and understand, imagine being the original recipients of the letter of Revelation who were going through great persecution from Rome, Pagans, and the Jews. It may be that God's design of reign in the present is very different from our understanding! We may need to remember Jesus' words, "I have told you these things so that in me you may have peace, in this world you will have trouble, but take heart, I have overcome the world." [LXVIII]

What is new about this song? This song could not have been sung before Jesus triumphed by the cross. Look at Isaiah 42:10-13 which predicted the Lord's triumph over his enemies and called for the singing of a new song when that happened. This is a song of glorious victory and the results thereof. It is a time of great rejoicing. But let's look at who else is singing.

MANY ANGELS

5:11, Then I looked and heard the voice of many angels, numbering thousands upon thousands, and ten thousand times ten thousand. They encircled the throne and, the living creatures, and the elders. 12, In a loud voice, they were saying:

"Worthy is the Lamb, who was slain, to receive power and wealth and wisdom and strength and honor and glory and praise!"

Here, we have an uncountable number of angels. Thousands upon thousands. Then ten thousand times ten thousand. Now we have our eyes opened to see that there is an even bigger circle around the throne of God, the circle of the four living creatures, and the circle of the 24 elders. There is a circle of so many angels that we can't quantify them. Verse 12 says something almost unnecessary. If you have that many angels saying something in unison, isn't it going to be loud? Yes, very. But the point must be made with authority. The Lamb who was slain is worthy. But worthy for what? He is worthy of receiving seven things. Remember, things of earth are represented by four attributes, and the things of God have three attributes. Therefore, Jesus, the one of heaven and earth, is spoken of with seven attributes.

EVERY CREATURE

5:13, Then I heard every creature in heaven and on earth and under the earth and on the sea, and all that is in them, saying:

"To him who sits on the throne and to the Lamb be praise and honor and glory and power, forever and ever!" 14, The four living creatures said, "Amen," and the elders fell down and worshiped.

First, we saw the 28 beings directly around God's throne worshipping the Lamb, then that expanded to a much bigger circle including an innumerable number of angels, now that circle is expanded again to include every creature in heaven and on earth and under the earth and on the sea and all that is in them. This must include unbelievers, right? Everyone gives praise, honor, glory, and power to the Lamb forever. Amazing. Interestingly, only the earthly nature of Jesus is highlighted in this part of the worship, as only four attributes are listed. Perhaps this is to correspond with the four divisions of creation.

GLORIOUS WORSHIP

Why are we shown this glorious worship? What purpose does showing us this worship serve to the overall message of Revelation? The people of the seven churches were going through a very tough time. They needed to know that God was in control and could take care of them. They needed to know how great, awesome, and mighty he was and always will be. To be assured that God knows who his people are and is able to bring them safely into his eternal kingdom.

Throughout these two chapters, we have noticed how God is described in groups of three attributes. Here is a summary of this amazing truth.

Table 7: Descriptions of God

1. The Father, the Son, the Holy Spirit.
2. Holy, Holy, Holy (4:8)
3. God who was, and is, and is to come (4:8)
4. Glory, honor, and thanks given to God (4:9)
5. Glory, honor, and power received by God (4:11)
6. Three groups of worshipers (5:9-10; 5:12; 5:13)
7. Three represents divinity.

The theme of Revelation is that all things glorious and beautiful are things we want to run to because they are righteous. The things that are dark, ugly, and scary are things we want to run away from because they are evil. It is through these pictures and ideas that they are planted deep in the emotional, picture-centered part of our brains, and they drive us toward the correct action.

CHAPTER 6

THE SCROLL AND SEVEN SEALS

Revelation 6:1 to 8:5.

So far, we've gone through five chapters of Revelation, and it has all been glorious and beautiful, except for the warnings to the churches if they aren't faithful. We are drawn to these things through righteousness because of faith. We will enjoy that beauty if we have and maintain the right relationship with God. We are about to see some very scary things that should have the result of pushing us away from the sin, evil, and corruption that leads to those disastrous things. We will discover God's ready judgment on evil and oppression. We will discover who can stand amid God's judgment, our purpose, and our care.

Some notes of caution as we head into this section of Revelation. We will see the much-ballyhooed Four Horses of the Apocalypse and experience our first visit with the 144,000. Please remember that these are visions. They are like scenes in a movie. We will see scenes in a series, but some scenes depict events that occur before or simultaneously with a previous scene. Also, they are signs - they don't have to make literal sense - they are used to getting a message across. Many people try to get more out of the text than the text wants to give. This may not be a great analogy, but it will get the point across: It's like trying to teach rocket science from a 2nd-grade math book. Revelation is not 2nd-grade literature, but let's be careful not to try to get more out of the text than we should.

THE FOUR SEALS AND FOUR HORSES

6:1, I watched as the Lamb opened the first of the seven seals. Then I heard one of the four living creatures say in a voice like thunder, "Come!" 2, I looked, and there before me was a white horse! Its rider held a bow, and he was given a crown, and he rode out as a conqueror bent on conquest. 3, When the Lamb opened the second seal, I heard the second living creature say, "Come!" 4, Then another horse came out, a fiery red one. Its rider was given the power to take peace from the earth and to make people kill each other. To him was given a large sword. 5, When the Lamb opened the third seal, I heard the third living creature say, "Come!" I looked, and there before me was a black horse! Its rider was holding a pair of scales in his hand. 6, Then I heard what sounded like a voice among the four living creatures, saying, "Two pounds of wheat for a day's wages, and six pounds of barley for a day's wages, and do not damage the oil and the wine!" 7, When the Lamb opened the fourth seal, I heard the voice of the fourth living creature say, "Come!" 8, I looked, and there before me was a pale horse! Its rider was named Death, and Hades was following close behind him. They were given power over a fourth of the earth to kill by sword, famine, and plague and by the wild beasts of the earth.

As John watches, the Lamb begins to open the seals. After the opening of each of the first four seals, one of the four living creatures gives the command in a voice like thunder. The command is simple and thunderous in its result. "Come." Each living creature gets a turn to issue the command, and after each command, a horse appears seemingly out of nowhere. There is incredible simplicity and power in this calling forth of the four horses.

WARS

The first horse is white, as purity. The rider has a bow and wears a victor's crown, not the crown of a king but the crown worn by someone victorious in war. That is why he rides like a conqueror bent on conquest. In every case in the Revelation, white signifies purity and holiness, so the white horse represents God's holy war. His judgment is on evil and oppression. The second horse is red. The rider has a large sword and the power to take peace from the earth. In so doing, he makes men slay each other as in civil war.

PESTILENCE

The third horse is black. The rider has a pair of scales and gives an exorbitant price for wheat and barley, but the oil and wine are not to be touched, giving us the idea of famine on a limited scale. The fourth horse is pale, like death. Of course, that's the rider's name, and he has Hades following close behind him. That makes sense. The place of the dead follows death. They kill one-quarter of the population through four pestilences: sword, famine, plague, and wild beasts. The death of one-quarter of the population seems extravagant, but it is still limited.

The four horses represent God's judgment on a world bent on persecuting Christians. We often see war, civil war, famine, and death from war, famine, plagues, and wild animals being used by God to judge evil nations. Here, we see a sequence of wars, even civil war, limited famine, and limited death coming by the sword, famine, plague, and wild beasts. This is the same sequence used by Jesus in a more general way in his prophecy of the destruction and judgment of Jerusalem. [LXIX] These things would have reminded Jewish readers of Ezekiel,[LXX] where he speaks of war, famine, plagues, and wild beasts as being the judgment of God.

Also, Jewish readers would have been reminded of Zechariah's four chariots, each with a team of horses.[LXXI] The horses have the same colors as those in Revelation, although they are not listed in the same sequence. Zechariah describes these chariots and their horses as the four spirits of heaven. They went out from standing in the presence of the Lord of the universe. When John saw the Lamb open each seal, it seemed that the horse and its rider simply appeared. But it is certain that they appeared out of the presence of the Lord of the entire world. This makes clear to us that they are under God's control. This should be a great comfort to the Christians who will see great turmoil in the world but know that God controls everything.

The message here is not said better than Robert Harkrider, who said, "Many are the modern references to 'the four horsemen' of this passage, but few understand that they rightfully declare the sovereignty of God. He permits the horsemen to ride. He controls them. He limits them. And he stops them when they have served their purpose."[LXXII]

THE FIFTH SEAL

6:9, When he opened the fifth seal, I saw under the altar the souls of those who had been slain because of the word of God and the testimony they had maintained. 10 They called out in a loud voice, "How long, Sovereign Lord, holy and true until you judge the inhabitants of the earth and avenge our blood?" 11, Then each of them was given a white robe, and they were told to wait a little longer until the full number of their fellow servants, their brothers and sisters, were killed just as they had been.

John sees a strange thing after the fifth seal is opened. He sees souls under the altar. These are identified as those who had been slain because of the word of God. They had given themselves up as sacrifices to God because of their testimony that they did not shrink in the face of death. While their location seems strange to us, it is a place of honor in God's economy. We can be sure of this because they have been given white robes to wear – they are pure and holy.

They are loudly calling for judgment on earth to begin against those who have caused their death. They are told to wait a little longer. More sacrifices must take place. More of their fellow servants of Christ must be martyred. This is where the idea of movie scenes becomes helpful in our understanding. The first four seals are God's answer to this event, which we see in the fifth seal. We will see more of this in the seventh seal.

THE SIXTH SEAL

6:12, I watched as he opened the sixth seal. There was a great earthquake. The sun turned black like sackcloth made of goat hair; the whole moon turned blood red, 13, and the stars in the sky fell to earth, as figs drop from a fig tree when shaken by a strong wind. 14, The heavens receded like a scroll being rolled up, and every mountain and island was removed from its place. 15, Then the kings of the earth, the princes, the generals, the rich, the mighty, and everyone else, both slave and free, hid in caves and among the rocks of the mountains. 16, They called to the mountains and the rocks, "Fall on us and hide us from the face of him who sits on the throne and from the wrath of the Lamb! 17, For the great day of their wrath has come, and who can withstand it?"

This looks a lot like the end of time judgment, with stars falling from the sky, the heavens receding like a scroll, and mountains and islands being removed from their places. But we see people hiding in caves and seeking big rocks for protection. Others call on mountains and rocks to fall on them to end their torment. But the point of this terrible vision is that when the Lamb's wrath comes upon mankind, can anyone withstand His judgment? Will anyone be found to be clear of His judgment? Remember the context of Revelation from the first chapter; these things must soon occur. There is going to be a timely judgment upon those who are persecuting Christians. Look at Isaiah 13:9-19 where God talks about the fall of Babylon that would soon occur in Isaiah's time. Also, read Isaiah 34:1-11, which shows a picture of God's judgment on all nations. These references in Isaiah are not end-times prophecies, as is clearly seen in Isaiah 34:11, where Isaiah says that animals will possess the judged land. The question is, when the Lamb's judgment comes, who can stand? Who CAN stand?

Before we move on from here, let's take a moment and think about what we, 2000 years removed from the author's intent, should get from the six seals. As I noted before, as described in the book The Ant and the Elephant, our cognitive brain is like an ant riding on an elephant, whereas the elephant is our emotional, picture-centered brain. We must use our cognitive brain to properly teach our emotional, picture-centered brain so that the elephant goes where the ant wants to go. Understand that these horrible pictures of the first six seals result from living outside of God's will. Teach yourself that you want to live in a manner in which God will be pleased so that you will not suffer the effects of the first six seals. Follow Paul's admonition and find out what pleases the Lord.[LXXIII] Then, do those things.

144,000 SEALED

7:1, After this, I saw four angels standing at the four corners of the earth, holding back the four winds of the earth to prevent any wind from blowing on the land or on the sea or on any tree. 2, Then I saw another angel coming up from the east, having the seal of the living God. He called out in a loud voice to the four angels who had been given power to harm the land and the sea: 3, "Do not harm the land or the sea or the trees until we put a seal on the foreheads of the servants of our God." 4, Then I heard the number of those who were sealed: 144,000 from all the tribes of Israel.

Revelation 7, verses 5-8 are summarized here: 12,000 each from the tribes of Judah, Reuben, Gad, Asher, Naphtali, Manasseh, Simeon, Levi, Issachar, Zebulun, Joseph, and Benjamin were sealed.

The question, "Who can stand?" asked by the fearful people after the sixth seal was opened, is about to be answered. John sees four angels standing at the four corners of the earth, holding back the four winds of the earth. Notice that the use of the number four references the things of the earth. Their power is to hold back the four winds. They receive a command from a fifth angel not to harm the earth until an event is complete, so we know that their purpose is to harm the earth. They are being restrained by God. They are under His control, and He has a limitation on His judgment. They are holding back the winds that will cause the earth's destruction until the correct time.

The fifth angel had the seal of the living God. He was going to seal those who are bondservants of our God. This seal was to go on their foreheads. After this was complete, then the four angels would be allowed to release the four winds. The reader should be reminded of Ezekiel.[LXXIV] Ezekiel sees a vision of a man putting a mark on the foreheads of the faithful in Jerusalem and six men following him and utterly killing everyone who did not have the mark. The promise is that if you are faithful to God, you will get the mark on your forehead and will not be killed in God's judgment. From what we see in Revelation 7 and Ezekiel 9, it must be clear that this mark is literal in the vision but not in reality.

However, the reader should also be reminded of a later passage in Ezekiel,[LXXV] where the judgment is spoken of differently. God says He will cut off from Jerusalem both the righteous and the wicked! What could possibly be the point? Whether they live or die, the righteous are exempt from the judgment about to take place on the earth.[LXXVI] Paul's words to Timothy ring out here,[LXXVII] 'Nevertheless, God's solid foundation stands firm, sealed with this inscription: "The Lord knows those who are his," and "Everyone who confesses the name of the Lord must turn away from wickedness."' Also, the Hebrew writer declares, [LXXVIII] "Therefore he is able to save completely those who come to God through him because he always lives to intercede for them."

The point here is that whether they live or die, God says, "All my saints are under my care! All of them!" Sealed people are authenticated as God's possession before going through the tribulation to come on earth. This was a tribulation to come soon to the original readers of Revelation. It was not some tribulation that would come some 2000 or more years later. However, we might also go through tribulations and must also take the same encouragement God sent to those in the first century.

But how does that work within the number of 144,000? Remember the numerology we talked about in the second chapter of this book? The number 12 is associated with the people of God. The number 1000 is a big number, standing for completeness. 12 times 12 times 1000 equals 144,000. Is this a literal number? Are there exactly 12,000 sealed from each of the 12 tribes of Israel that are listed? Notice that Joseph is listed along with one of his sons, Manasseh. Usually, if one of Joseph's sons is listed, then the other is also listed, and Joseph is not. Levi is listed, although sometimes, in the Old Testament, Levi stands apart because they served in the temple and did not receive a land inheritance. But this arrangement means there is no room for the tribe of Dan. Now, back to the question: is 144,000 a literal number? If 144,000 is literal, then the number of people sealed must be literally from each of the tribes listed and be exactly 12,000 each. If 144,000 is literal, then so are the four angels holding back the wind. Besides, if 144,000 is literal, what will we do with the great multitude of verse 9? I suggest that 144,000 is not literal, nor are the tribe names.

THE GREAT MULTITUDE

7:9, After this, I looked, and there before me was a great multitude that no one could count, from every nation, tribe, people, and language, standing before the throne and before the Lamb. They were wearing white robes and were holding palm branches in their hands. 10 And they cried out in a loud voice: "Salvation belongs to our God, who sits on the throne, and to the Lamb."

Look back at Revelation 4:2 and notice where John is standing. He is standing such that the throne is before him. Now we see a great multitude standing before him, the throne, and the Lamb. What is most important to notice is that this great multitude, not to mention John, was standing. As if in answer to the question, "Who can stand?" posed by those in terror at the judgments we've just seen, we have this great multitude standing. This multitude is dressed in white robes, and they are holding palm branches. We already know that since they were wearing white robes, they were pure and holy. If you think back to the triumphal entry of Jesus into Jerusalem, you will remember that at that event, the people were waving palm branches, symbolizing joy and triumph. Palm branches were waved during the parade of a conquering army when it returned to Rome to celebrate its victory and receive its reward. Palm branches were also used at the feast of the Tabernacles when they thanked God for the ingathered fruits.

In verse 14, we see that this great multitude came out of the great tribulation. Now, the 144,000 were those who were sealed before the great tribulation. In John's vision, 144,000 people were sealed on earth, and the innumerable multitude was in heaven. So, the great multitude is all the marked people who went through the tribulation and are now in heaven. Therefore, 144,000 from the tribes of Israel are figurative representations. As Paul said in the letter to the Romans,[LXXIX] the gospel is for the Jews first, then the

Gentiles. That is why we see the 144,000 Jews first and then see the people from every nation, tribe, people, and language. Notice again the use of four attributes pertaining to things of the earth.

The great multitude, which is the 144,000, worship God who sits on the throne and the Lamb, saying, "Salvation belongs" to them. God and the Lamb are equivalent in our salvation.

7:11 All the angels were standing around the throne and around the elders and the four living creatures. They fell down on their faces before the throne and worshiped God, 12, saying: "Amen! Praise and glory and wisdom and thanks and honor and power and strength be to our God forever and ever. Amen!"

Now added to the multitude that no one could count are all the angels and the four living creatures. They are all worshipping God together. A significant point is being made here. While the redeemed people of the earth stood to worship God, the angels and four living creatures fell on their faces in the worship of God. Is this because those redeemed from the earth are greater than the angels? No. The point is being doubly emphasized that they can stand before God Almighty. God's judgment is not meant for them, and we'll see why in the next section.

7:13, Then one of the elders asked me, "These in white robes—who are they, and where did they come from?" 14, I answered, "Sir, you know." And he said, "These are they who have come out of the great tribulation; they have washed their robes and made them white in the blood of the Lamb. 15, Therefore, "they are before the throne of God and serve Him day and night in His temple, and He who sits on the throne will shelter them with His presence. 16, 'Never again will they hunger; never again will they thirst. The sun will not beat down on them, nor any scorching heat. 17, For the

Lamb at the center of the throne, will be their shepherd; 'He will lead them to springs of living water.' 'And God will wipe away every tear from their eyes.'"

As we pointed out above, this great multitude dressed in white robes came out of great tribulation. The 144,000 were sealed going into the great tribulation, and this multitude beyond number has come out of it. They have washed their robes and made them white in the blood of the Lamb. The only way this happens is through repentance, obedience to God in baptism, [LXXX] and living in faithful obedience to his will – walking in the light. [LXXXI] For this reason (verse 15 above), they are before the throne of God and serve Him day and night in His temple. They are able to stand before the God of their salvation. God shelters them, and the Lamb shepherds them. Isn't that ironic? A lamb as a shepherd? But that's how God does things! Because of God's shelter, they are never hungry, thirsty, or overheated. Because the Lamb shepherds them, they get plenty of living water. And God has removed sorrow from their hearts and replaced it with eternal joy – the tears are wiped away.

Think again about the statement that "they have washed their robes and made them white in the blood of the lamb." Never let anyone tell you we don't have a part in our own salvation! We do. The result is that we are under God's fourfold care,

1. Never hungry

2. Never thirsty

3. Never sun-burnt

4. Always comforted.

This section ends with a message of hope! Regardless of the turmoil, persecution, and death that are all around us, God is in control. He knows those who are His and is able to bring them safely through. Consider this seventh chapter of Revelation as an invitation to stand. Choose to meditate on this beautiful picture so that you are driven toward the actions and lifestyle that will move you in a way that will ensure that this result will be true for you. Now, let's see what happens when the seventh seal is opened. I think you'll be amazed!

THE SEVENTH SEAL

8:1, When he opened the seventh seal, there was silence in heaven for about half an hour. 2, And I saw the seven angels who stand before God, and seven trumpets were given to them. 3, Another angel, who had a golden censor, came and stood at the altar. He was given much incense to offer, with the prayers of all God's people, on the golden altar in front of the throne. 4, The smoke of the incense, together with the prayers of God's people, went up before God from the angel's hand. 5, Then the angel took the censer, filled it with fire from the altar, and hurled it on the earth; and there came peals of thunder, rumblings, flashes of lightning, and an earthquake.

Okay. I feel obliged to tell a joke here: Do you know why there was silence in heaven for a half hour? Apparently, there were no women in heaven for that half hour. I know. Bad joke.

There is Silence in heaven for about half an hour because something momentous is about to happen. Seven angels who stand before God are given seven trumpets, one for each angel. They are preparing for the seven trumpets to come. They announced that the seven seals were warnings, and they were complete. Much more, they announce the judgment that is coming. We'll see what those trumpets signify in chapters 8 through 11 of Revelation.

But the momentous thing is what happens next. Another angel comes forward with a golden censor and much incense to offer on the altar before the throne. God sits facing this altar. All His attention is focused on the altar. The angel puts the contents of his censor on the altar, and smoke rises from the incense. What I really find so momentous about this scene is that the prayers of God's people are mixed in with the incense. The prayers of the saints are a sacrifice to God and are given his supreme attention. The word "saints" does not signify some super-Christian. Saints are the people of God. Christians. If you are in Christ, you are a saint. God's attention is set on the sacrifice of your prayers and the prayers of all of God's people.

What is even more momentous is the results of those prayers offered by the people of God, us, the saints. Let me repeat verse 5 here: *Then the angel took the censer, filled it with fire from the altar, and hurled it on the earth; and there came peals of thunder, rumblings, flashes of lightning, and an earthquake.* The judgment on evil results from the prayers of God's people who are being persecuted for following Christ. When you see turmoil on earth, it just might be God's judgment on wicked people because of the prayers of the saints asking God to deal with their wickedness. We must be serious about our prayers, knowing that God gives them such attention and will answer our prayers. God's judgment here, shown in Revelation, is a response to the prayers of the saints! Amazing!

Now, we will see what the seven trumpets call up.

CHAPTER 7

THE SEVEN TRUMPETS

Revelation 8:6 to 11:19.

The purpose of all these seals and now the trumpets is to call people to repent. In fact, the express intent of the trumpets is to call people to repent. God is committed to His covenant with his people. God is not negligent in this matter. God is very protective of those who are in a covenant relationship with Him and will enact severe judgment on those who would hurt his people, the body of His son. While we hear the seven trumpets, we will also see a little book, observe the measuring of the temple, and see what happens to God's two witnesses. This will be exciting. This will be motivating.

THE FOUR TRUMPETS

8:6, Then the seven angels who had the seven trumpets prepared to sound them. 7, The first angel sounded his trumpet, and there came hail and fire mixed with blood, and it was hurled down on the earth. A third of the earth was burned up, a third of the trees were burned up, and all the green grass was burned up. 8, The second angel sounded his trumpet, and something like a huge mountain, all ablaze, was thrown into the sea. A third of the sea turned into blood. 9, A third of the living creatures in the sea died, and a third of the ships were destroyed. 10, The third angel sounded his trumpet, and a great star, blazing like a torch, fell from the sky on a third of the rivers and on the springs of water— 11, The name of the star is Wormwood. A third of the waters turned bitter, and many people died from the waters that had become bitter. 12, The fourth angel sounded his trumpet, and a third of the sun was struck, a third of the moon, and a third of the stars so that a third of them turned dark. A third of the day was without light, and also a third of the night.

Trumpets are often used to call people to attention and to sound a warning. This is certainly the intention of their use here. It is important to understand that this is still a vision that John is seeing. These things are not literally happening in the physical world. We are being called to attention and warned of the fate of those who turn away from God and treat the people of God with contempt.

THE FIRST TRUMPET

The first trumpet hurls hail and fire down on the earth. They don't just fall on the earth. They are hurled down on the earth. If that isn't enough, they are mixed with blood. One-third of the earth and trees are burned up, and all the green grass is burned up. The first trumpet destroyed much vegetation and seriously affected the food supply. The judgment is limited, however. God is holding back full retribution.

THE SECOND TRUMPET

The second trumpet throws what looks like a huge mountain into the sea. A third of the sea turns to blood, a third of the sea creatures die, and a third of the ships are destroyed. As frightening as this is, the judgment is limited. This judgment affects the naval power and the shipping industry.

THE THIRD TRUMPET

The third trumpet sends a great star falling from the sky onto the rivers and springs of water. The star is blazing like a torch and is called Wormwood, which is a bitter substance. It turns all the water that it affects bitter, and many people die in agony from using the bitter water. Again, we see that this judgment is limited as it affects only one-third of the freshwater sources. This judgment affects the freshwater supply and related industries.

THE FOURTH TRUMPET

The fourth trumpet causes darkness where there should be light. One-third of the sun has turned dark. One-third of the moon has turned dark. One-third of the stars are blotted out. Now, one-third of the day is dark, and one-third of the night has no light at all. This judgment affects the heavens and how we experience life on earth.

Does this scare you? Remember what the cause of all this judgment is? It is the answer to the prayers of the saints. Read again verses 4 and 5 of Revelation 8. Whatever disaster happens here on earth should not scare you if you are one of God's people. God has you in His eternal care. You may go through great suffering on earth, maybe even cause your death, but God will give you the crown of life. Let these things scare you into Jesus' arms. He will lead you beside quiet waters, even when the world is chaotic.

How do we interpret these events? It must be in the context of the writing of the book of Revelation to the people suffering persecution near the end of the first century AD. The center of that persecution was Rome, and many details in Revelation can be used to point in Rome's direction. In Jeremiah,[LXXXII] Babylon is called a burned-out mountain, as in the second trumpet. Isaiah[LXXXIII] speaks of Babylon's king and how he would fall from his "heavenly" position and be cast down to the earth, as in the third trumpet. Babylon had conquered the nations and would itself be laid low. As we move forward in Revelation, we'll see that Babylon is spoken of as causing the persecution of God's people. At the time of the first century, Babylon was not a concern, so it appears that Babylon was code for those who were causing the persecution of Christians centered in Rome. As an empire, Rome did not fall until 476 A.D., so this is not directly speaking of the fall of Rome. Domitian, the figurehead of the persecution, was assassinated on September 18, 96 A.D.

Most importantly, God responds to His people when they cry out to Him. Many examples of this can be seen throughout scripture, and God has not changed. These things, whether they have been fulfilled in the past, never to be fulfilled again, or there is future fulfillment yet to come, are judgments on those who persecute God's people. Even if God's people are physically caught up in the judgment, their hope is in God, their salvation is in Christ, and their home is in heaven.

THE FIFTH TRUMPET AND THE FIRST WOE

8:13, As I watched, I heard an eagle that was flying in midair call out in a loud voice: "Woe! Woe! Woe to the inhabitants of the earth because of the trumpet blasts about to be sounded by the other three angels!"

9:1, The fifth angel sounded his trumpet, and I saw a star that had fallen from the sky to the earth. The star was given the key to the shaft of the Abyss. 2, When he opened the Abyss, smoke rose from it like the smoke from a gigantic furnace. The sun and sky were darkened by the smoke from the Abyss. 3, And out of the smoke, locusts came down on the earth and were given power like that of scorpions of the earth. 4, They were told not to harm the grass of the earth or any plant or tree, but only those people who did not have the seal of God on their foreheads. 5, They were not allowed to kill them but only to torture them for five months. And the agony they suffered was like that of the sting of a scorpion when it strikes. 6, During those days, people will seek death but will not find it; they will long to die, but death will elude them. 7, The locusts looked like horses prepared for battle. On their heads, they wore something like crowns of gold, and their faces resembled human faces. 8, Their hair was like women's hair, and their teeth were like lions' teeth. 9, They had breastplates like breastplates of iron, and the sound of their wings was like the thundering of many horses and chariots rushing into battle. 10, They had tails with stingers, like scorpions, and in their tails, they had the power to torment people for five months. 11, They had as king over them the angel of the Abyss, whose name in Hebrew is Abaddon and in Greek is Apollyon (that is, Destroyer). 12, The first woe is past; two other woes are yet to come.

Before the fifth angel sounds his trumpet, an eagle is seen flying through the air and speaking in John's language! The angel cries "woe" three times, one for each of the remaining trumpet blasts to be sounded. The woes to come are upon the inhabitants of the earth. These woes are not upon God's people, the saints. The saints, Christians, dwell in heaven even while living on earth. See Ephesians 2:6, "*And God raised us up with Christ and seated us with him in the heavenly realms in Christ Jesus.*"

Here, at the sound of the fifth trumpet, we see a star fall from the sky, just as at the sound of the third trumpet. The difference between these two stars and the star of Isaiah 14 is that these two stars fall at the command of God, are under his control, and are doing his will to bring judgment on those who do evil. The star of Isaiah 14 fell because of judgment upon Babylon. The star of the fifth trumpet is given the key to the shaft of the Abyss. Who gave him the key? God did. God has control over the Abyss, and He controls who goes in and out of it and when they do so.

The star opens the Abyss, and so much smoke rises from it that the sun and sky are darkened. The sun and sky had already lost 1/3 of their brightness in the fourth trumpet; now, they are further darkened by the smoke of the Abyss. Locusts come out of the smoke, but these locusts don't eat grass and green plants – they harm people. But they only harm those who do not have the seal of God on their foreheads.

Incidentally, if you believe in The Rapture, how do you explain this? What are the people of God doing on earth during this tribulation? Weren't they raptured? We know that if there are no Christians here, then people can't be taught about Christ, for God always uses people to teach people. Remember

Paul's words, LXXXIV *"How, then, can they call on the one they have not believed in? And how can they believe in the one whom they have not heard? And how can they hear without someone preaching to them? And how can anyone preach unless they are sent? As it is written: 'How beautiful are the feet of those who bring good news!'"* So, there is no rapture before Jesus' final return.

Again, the point is that God's people, the saints, A.K.A. Christians, are exempt from this tribulation. Those who are not God's people do not have the seal of God on their forehead. These are the people that get stung by these scorpion-like locusts. Their purpose is to cause agony, but it is limited to five months. But five months of torture is a long time! It is so painful, and it seems like it will never end that those so inflicted seek death but are not able to obtain it. That's where the real torture comes in.

At first, when you see one of these locusts, you are attracted to them. They have human faces and women's hair – apparently done up really pretty. And they have a beautiful crown of gold on their heads. When you see them closer, you realize your mistake. They look like horses going into battle with breastplates of iron. Then they open their mouths, and you see the lion's teeth. This is a physical representation of how sin affects those who give themselves over to it. Sin causes the one who seeks its pleasures to be tortured in their soul. Evil is deceptive – it looks pleasurable and attractive, but its effect is torture.

Do these things scare you? Then, flee from sin and the temptations of this world. As Paul instructed Timothy, LXXXV *"Flee the evil desires of youth and pursue righteousness, faith, love, and peace, along with those who call on the Lord out of a pure heart."* The source of sin's torture is from the locusts of the Abyss, whose king is Abaddon, Apollyon, the Destroyer! This is clearly Satan, the star that fell from heaven to whom God gave the key to the Abyss, who opened the Abyss, releasing such terror upon the people of the earth. So, Satan finds himself doing the will of God to judge those who do Satan's work. Satan's hatred for God's creation provokes him to do God's will because, as we will see shortly, the purpose of all these woes is that people would turn from their wicked ways and seek the Lord while he may be found.

THE SIXTH TRUMPET AND THE SECOND WOE

9:13, The sixth angel sounded his trumpet, and I heard a voice coming from the four horns of the golden altar that is before God. 14, It said to the sixth angel who had the trumpet, "Release the four angels who are bound at the great river Euphrates." 15, And the four angels who had been kept ready for this very hour and day and month and year were released to kill a third of mankind. 16, The number of the mounted troops was twice ten thousand times ten thousand. I heard their number. 17, The horses and riders I saw in my vision looked like this: Their breastplates were fiery red, dark blue, and yellow as sulfur. The heads of the horses resembled the heads of lions, and out of their mouths came fire, smoke, and sulfur. 18, A third of mankind was killed by the three plagues of fire, smoke, and sulfur that came out of their mouths. 19, The power of the horses was in their mouths and in their tails, for their tails were like snakes, having heads with which they inflict injury. 20, The rest of mankind who were not killed by these plagues still did not repent of the work of their hands; they did not stop worshiping demons and idols of gold, silver, bronze, stone, and wood—idols that cannot see or hear or walk. 21, Nor did they repent of their murders, their magic arts, their sexual immorality, or their thefts.

At the sound of the sixth trumpet, a voice came from the four horns of the golden altar before God. The voice calls for the release of four angels bound until this moment. Their purpose is to kill a third of mankind. The voice came from the altar. What was put on the altar? Incense, with the prayers of God's people. This is happening as God's answer to the prayers of God's people! Are you one of God's people? Have you been put into Christ through baptism prompted by faith? Then, this event is not to your harm. But it should motivate us to try to persuade those who are in harm's way to turn their lives over to the Lord.

After the sixth seal, [LXXXVI] we saw four angels at the four corners of the earth who were not allowed to harm anything. They were holding back the winds that would bring destruction. Now, at the sixth trumpet, we see four angels released to bring judgment on mankind. We saw the warning of judgment, and now we see the enactment of judgment. As devastating as it is, it is limited to one-third of the population. Notice again the unity of God's word; these four angels were prepared for this hour, day, month, and year - four attributes referencing things related to creation.

Doing the math, these angels released 200 million mounted troops. The fifth trumpet released scorpion-like locusts to torture people for five months, but they could not kill anyone. Now, after that is complete, the 200 million mounted troops are released, but they are commanded to kill. Still, they are limited in the number of killings they may do. God is always in control.

These horses, being ridden by fearsome riders, are more fearsome than the riders. They have the heads of lions that act like dragons, billowing fire, smoke, and brimstone coming out of their mouths, while their tails are like serpents, with serpent's heads to inflict harm. The horses do harm from both their heads and their tails and kill one-third of mankind.

What did the people of Earth do in response to all this devastation, those who were not killed by these plagues? They did not repent! That was the whole point of all this terrible judgment – to get people to repent. But they would not. The works of their hands were for the purpose of worshipping demons and idols made of gold, silver, brass, stone, and wood.

They refused to stop worshipping powerless things. Things that had no ability to help them overcome the plagues by which they were inflicted. They continued in their four (notice again the earthly reference) sins: murders, witchcraft, sexual immorality, and theft.

Do these things scare you? Is this not terrible to think about? Then, do not be like the people of Earth who refuse to repent of their sins. This is the point of all these terrible things: to motivate repentance. Turn away from wickedness and turn to God. Let him teach you righteousness.

AN ANGEL AND A LITTLE OPEN BOOK

10:1, Then I saw another mighty angel coming down from heaven. He was robed in a cloud, with a rainbow above his head; his face was like the sun, and his legs were like fiery pillars. 2, He was holding a little scroll, which lay open in his hand. He planted his right foot on the sea and his left foot on the land, 3, and he gave a loud shout like the roar of a lion. When he shouted, the voices of the seven thunders spoke. 4, And when the seven thunders spoke, I was about to write; but I heard a voice from heaven say, "Seal up what the seven thunders have said and do not write it down." 5, Then the angel I had seen standing on the sea and on the land raised his right hand to heaven. 6, And he swore by him who lives forever and ever, who created the heavens and all that is in them, the earth and all that is in it, and the sea and all that is in it, and said, "There will be no more delay! 7, But in the days when the seventh angel is about to sound his trumpet, the mystery of God will be accomplished, just as he announced to his servants the prophets." 8, Then the voice that I had heard from heaven spoke to me once more: "Go, take the scroll that lies open in the hand of the angel who is standing on the sea and on the land." 9, So I went to the angel and asked him to give me the little scroll. He said to me, "Take it and eat it. It will turn your stomach sour, but 'in your mouth, it will be as sweet as honey.'" 10, I took the little scroll from the angel's hand and ate it. It tasted as sweet as honey in my mouth, but when I had eaten it, my stomach turned sour. 11, Then I was told, "You must prophesy again about many peoples, nations, languages, and kings."

Remember that after the sixth seal, there was an interlude before the seventh seal was opened.[LXXXVII] Now, after the sixth trumpet, there is an interlude before the seventh trumpet.[LXXXVIII]

THE ANGEL AND THE SEVEN THUNDERS

Here, we see not just any angel. This is a mighty angel. He is wearing a robe that is a cloud of glory and has a rainbow above his head. Certainly, the rainbow harkens to the thoughts of the rainbow God showed Noah when He promised never to destroy the earth again with a flood. This represents the mercy and covenant-keeping reliability of God. This angel has a beautiful glowing face. Of course, his face shines like the sun! Everyone who is in God's presence has this result. His legs are like fiery pillars which he plants on the earth. He does not just come down and stand – he plants his feet with authority. This is amazing power and even more so when one foot is planted on the sea and the other on land. This angel's appearance must be a reminder of Moses, whose face shown after time with God and who was protected by a pillar of fire along with all the other Israelites in their 40-year trek in the wilderness.

THE SEVEN THUNDERS

This powerful angel does something quite unexpected. But by now, John must be getting used to the unexpected. The angel gives a loud shout that sounds like a lion's roar. Imagine what that must be like. Then, to have that shout backed up by the voices of *the* seven thunders. We aren't told, and we cannot imagine what the Seven Thunders said. We are told there will be no more delays, so we can assume that whatever the seven thunders said there would have caused a delay. That is why they were sealed up.

We saw the seven seals, which revealed the coming judgment, and then the seven trumpets, which warned of the coming judgment. Now we've been told there were seven thunders, but no time has been taken to tell us what they were about. The seals affected one-quarter of the earth. The trumpets affected one-third of the earth. Maybe the seven thunders would have affected one-half of the earth. When we see the seven bowls later, we'll see no limit to the area they affect.

THE OATH

The angel that had planted his feet on the earth and on the sea firmly now raises his right hand to heaven to make an oath. He swears by him who:

i.   Lives forever and ever.

ii.   Created the heavens and all that is in them.

iii.   Created the earth and all that is in it.

iv.   Created the sea and all that is in it.

God has four attributes here because we are focusing on his creation. Creation has four attributes. When the seventh trumpet sounds, the mystery of God will be accomplished. This mystery has been announced by God's servants, the prophets, for thousands of years. Finally, there is no more delay. The mystery will be carried out. We aren't waiting for the seven thunders; we will get to it soon!

THE BOOK

When the angel came down from heaven, we saw an open scroll in his hand. The scroll is small because John must eat it. The voice that John has been hearing from heaven, which has been telling him what to do, now tells him to take the scroll from the angel. This he does, but the angel tells him to take it and eat it. He is told, "It will be sweet as honey, but it will upset your tummy." And, of course, it is and does. The book is the word of God. Maybe its small size means that it is a limited message. John must eat the book, just as we must eat the word of God to master it, completely understand it, and be transformed by its message. Mastering God's word is sweet, but in this case, the message is full of woe, so it is bitter to the stomach.

THE TWO WITNESSES

11:1, I was given a reed like a measuring rod and was told, "Go and measure the temple of God and the altar, with its worshipers. 2, But exclude the outer court; do not measure it, because it has been given to the Gentiles. They will trample on the holy city for 42 months. 3, And I will appoint my two witnesses, and they will prophesy for 1,260 days, clothed in sackcloth." 4, They are "the two olive trees" and the two lampstands, and "they stand before the Lord of the earth." 5, If anyone tries to harm them, fire comes from their mouths and devours their enemies. This is how anyone who wants to harm them must die. 6, They have the power to shut up the heavens so that it will not rain during the time they are prophesying, and they have the power to turn the waters into blood and to strike the earth with every kind of plague as often as they want. 7, Now, when they have finished their testimony, the beast that comes up from the Abyss will attack them and overpower and kill them. 8, Their bodies will lie in the public square of the great city—which is figuratively called Sodom and Egypt—where also their Lord was crucified. 9, For three and a half days, some from every people, tribe, language, and nation will gaze on their bodies and refuse them burial. 10, The inhabitants of the earth will gloat over them and will celebrate by sending each other gifts because these two prophets had tormented those who live on the earth. 11, But after the three and a half days, the breath of life from God entered them, and they stood on their feet, and terror struck those who saw them. 12, Then they heard a loud voice from heaven saying to them, "Come up here." And they went up to heaven in a cloud, while their enemies looked on. 13, At that very hour, there was a severe earthquake, and a tenth of the city collapsed. Seven thousand people were killed in the earthquake, and the survivors were terrified and gave glory to the God of heaven. 14, The second woe has passed; the third woe is coming soon.

John is given a reed like a measuring rod, a clear representation of the standard of truth. He measures the temple of God, the altar, and the people worshipping there. All these items are holy as they meet the standard of measurement. Those things that are not measured, such as the outer court, are profane as they do not meet the standard of measurement. The book of Ezekiel[LXXXIX] tells of the rebuilding of the Jew's physical temple many years after it had been destroyed by Nebuchadnezzar. Ezekiel, whom God calls the "son of man," sees a man measure the temple in great detail. In this case, it includes the outer court. When all the temple is found to meet the measurement standard, God's glory fills the temple. In John's vision, however, the spiritual temple is being measured. The temple is the faithful church, true Israel, which includes both Jews and Gentiles. [XC] The altar receives the church's prayers, and those who worship there are the faithful members of the church.

Those in the outer court, outside the measured area, are characterized as Gentiles or nations – as distinct from Israel. They are outside the church; they are not true Israel because they are not God's people. These people include unfaithful Christians. They will trample on the holy city, otherwise known as the church. This may either mean that they are persecuting the church, that they are worshiping God in a false manner, or both. In Isaiah's first chapter, God chastised rebellious Israel for acting like they were worshipping God when there was blood on their hands. He asks them why they are trampling his courts when he wants worship from people whose lives are congruent with their worship.

They will trample the holy city for 42 months. During this same length of time, probably concurrently, God's two witnesses will prophesy. 42 months is equivalent to 1260 days or 3.5 years. This is not a specific timeframe, but it is a short period in which the people of God would endure this persecution.

These two witnesses will be killed at the end of the 1260 days, and their bodies will be left in the square of the city figuratively called Sodom and Egypt. Sodom was testified against by two witnesses,[XCI] the angels that rescued Lot and his daughters. Egypt was testified against by two witnesses,[XCII] Moses and Aaron. The two witnesses of Revelation are clothed in sackcloth, the Old Testament symbol of suffering, mourning, and sorrow. They have sorrow because of the sins of the people that they are witnessing against. They are described as olive trees and lampstands. Olive trees symbolized fruitfulness, abundance, and blessing to Israel, and olive oil was used to honor kings. In every case where we've seen candlesticks so far, they have represented the church. These two witnesses, then, represent the faithful church. They might specifically represent Smyrna and Philadelphia, the only cities Jesus had no reproof.

There are several places in scripture where we see two witnesses. Which two witnesses are being referred to in Revelation? Here are some of the options:

1.   Two angels against Sodom.

2.   Moses and Aaron against Egypt.

3.   Anointed kings and priests.

4.   Two faithful churches, Smyrna and Philadelphia.

5.   OT and NT.

6.   Moses and Elijah: Law and Prophets.

The two witnesses speak to the strength of their witness against the evil perpetrated against God's people. Remember that these events are God's answer to the prayers of his tormented people. In the Old Covenant, a person could not be condemned without the witness of at least two people. There could be no better explanation of the description of these two witnesses than Zechariah 4. In Zechariah's vision, he saw two olive trees, a lampstand of one base, and seven channels to seven lights that represent faithful Israel. Here in John's vision, the seven separate lampstands represent the faithful church. When Zechariah asked his guide what the lampstand and olive trees were, he was told, "*This is the word of the LORD to Zerubbabel: 'Not by might nor by power, but by my Spirit,' says the LORD Almighty.*" In Zechariah's case, the two olive trees were witnesses who were anointed to serve the Lord of all the earth just as these two witnesses "stand before the Lord of the earth." Since Zechariah's two witnesses were anointed, they represent kings and priests because a person was anointed by olive oil upon entering these offices. This again points to God's faithful people since Jesus made us a kingdom and priests to serve God, and thus, we are a royal priesthood.[XCIII]

These witnesses were untouchable until their witness was complete. God is going to make sure he gets His message across and that it has the effect that it is intended to have. Their words burn like fire, and they can bring the plagues that the angels brought to Sodom and Moses and Aaron to Egypt. Just as the apostles' word was confirmed by miracles, so these two witnesses have their words confirmed as being God's word by the miracles they performed. But when they have completed their mission, then God allows Satan to win. Temporarily. As Satan got to gloat over Jesus for 3 days, he got to gloat over these two witnesses for 3.5 days. But all gloating is short-lived with a terrible end.

But wait, did you see where the bodies of the two witnesses lay in state? Verse 8, *Their bodies will lie in the public square of the great city – which is figuratively called Sodom and Egypt – where also their Lord was crucified*. We already spoke of Sodom and Egypt above, but that is what the city is *figuratively* known as. This is Jerusalem, where Jesus was crucified. Why is Jerusalem not specifically named but only alluded to? The point would seem to be that there may be many repetitions of events like these throughout history. There may be many cities that are figuratively known as Sodom and Egypt where God's faithful witnesses will preach God's confirmed word and suffer persecution even to death. But in every case, Satan's victory is short-lived. But while he has it, his people will celebrate. These people of the earth, from every people, tribe, language, and nation, four attributes, will think of it as a sport to gaze at their bodies, to gloat over them, and to celebrate by sending each other gifts. How grotesque we become because of our sins!

But to borrow from a wonderful song, "It's only Friday; Sunday is coming!" God restores His faithful witnesses to life, and they stand on their feet. Satan and his people only get to enjoy the victory for a brief time before they are again struck with terror as they see once again that they cannot defeat God and his purpose and his people. God calls them up to heaven; like Jesus, they ascend to heaven in a cloud. This time, however, the enemies look on. Now, the sixth trumpet is completed with further devastation brought about by a severe earthquake. One-tenth of the city is destroyed, and seven thousand people are killed. Again, we have the limitation on judgment and the sign of its completeness. Seven and ten are both representations of completeness, but they are phrased in such a way to show that God is still limiting the judgment. In this case, the survivors gave glory to the God of heaven, showing the success of God's judgment. The second woe is passed, resulting in the people of Earth giving glory to God. It leads to the seventh trumpet, in which we see the worship of God again.

THE SEVENTH TRUMPET AND THE THIRD WOE

11:15, The seventh angel sounded his trumpet, and there were loud voices in heaven, which said:

> "The kingdom of the world has become
> the kingdom of our Lord and of his Messiah,
> and he will reign forever and ever."

16, And the twenty-four elders, who were seated on their thrones before God, fell on their faces and worshiped God, 17 saying:

> "We give thanks to you, Lord God Almighty,
> the One who is and who was,
> because you have taken your great power
> and have begun to reign.
> 18 The nations were angry,
> and your wrath has come.
> The time has come for judging the dead,
> and for rewarding your servants, the prophets
> and your people who revere your name,
> both great and small—
> and for destroying those who destroy the earth."

19, Then God's temple in heaven was opened, and within his temple was seen the ark of his covenant. And there came flashes of lightning, rumblings, peals of thunder, an earthquake, and a severe hailstorm.

Finally! The seventh angel sounds his trumpet. Remember again, the reason for the seven trumpets was the prayers of the saints. They were asking for judgment against those who were causing their suffering. That is what we saw through the first six trumpets, the prophecies of John from the little book he ate, and the two witnesses, culminating in the great earthquake. The point of all this judgment is to bring people to repentance,[XCIV] which the earthquake survivors did.[XCV] So, the voices in heaven praise God for the success of God's judgment.

The kingdom of the world has become the kingdom of our Lord and of his Messiah. The Messiah will reign forever and ever. But wait, isn't this what happened at Jesus' resurrection? Yes. And it is being recognized, emphasized, and reinforced at the two witnesses' resurrection.

The mystery of God is finished. Death has been swallowed up in victory. The death of the Messiah was God's plan for the salvation of all Jews and Gentiles who believe. God and Jesus are now reigning without contest. Satan and his servants have been shown to be powerless frauds and have failed as they are doomed to do forever. Those who remain faithful to God are vindicated, and those who are unfaithful are punished. In the end, we see that the way to God's temple in heaven is opened. The ark of the covenant is visible. We can have direct access to God through the atoning death of our Lord Jesus Christ. Yes, there are flashes of lightning, rumblings, peals of thunder, earthquakes, and a severe hailstorm, but they somehow have lost their fearfulness. Wonder, amazement, and understanding of the protective power of God have replaced those emotions. We now stand awed by the One who saved, protected, loved, redeemed, made a way for us, and brought us home to be with Him. The emotions that are left are those of a desire to please Him - a desire to hold on to Him at all costs. Letting all fear and doctrines of men and whatever else would come between us and our Lord go and fall by the wayside.

Just one more quick thematic note: The first four trumpets, as are the first four seals, are short in their descriptions. They indirectly affect man but magnificently display God's control over His world. The last three trumpets each have a lengthy, detailed description and directly affect man. They magnificently display God's sovereignty over the people of the earth. He expresses his anger toward the people who choose evil and his care of those who obey and worship Him in spirit and in truth. He displays his SEMPER FI attitude toward his covenant.

CHAPTER 8

THE SEVEN-HEADED DRAGON

Revelation 12:1 to 12:17.

As we finished the seven trumpets, we saw that God's call for people to repent still stands. In fact, the purpose of the earthly difficulties is to get us to repent. In this chapter, we will see how much Satan hates Christ and the church and see, once again, God's victory over Satan. But what does a seven-headed dragon do when it can't defeat a pregnant woman? Let's find out!

THE WOMAN AND THE DRAGON

12:1, A great sign appeared in heaven: a woman clothed with the sun, with the moon under her feet and a crown of twelve stars on her head. 2, She was pregnant and cried out in pain as she was about to give birth. 3, Then another sign appeared in heaven: an enormous red dragon with seven heads and, ten horns, and seven crowns on its heads. 4, Its tail swept a third of the stars out of the sky and flung them to the earth. The dragon stood in front of the woman who was about to give birth so that it might devour her child the moment he was born. 5, She gave birth to a son, a male child, who "will rule all the nations with an iron scepter." And her child was snatched up to God and to His throne. 6, The woman fled into the wilderness to a place prepared for her by God, where she might be taken care of for 1,260 days.

This is the first time the word "sign" has been used to describe what John saw. A sign is an indicator of some feature or event that is behind it or something you will come upon if you persist in the direction you are going. A sign is not reality but represents some feature of reality. So, what is a great sign? It must be a sign of something that has a significant impact. It

95

must be an unusually large sign that you just can't miss. But this great sign only takes two verses to describe. First, the woman is clothed with the sun, the moon is under her feet, and she has a crown of twelve stars on her head. Every time someone has the appearance of the sun, they have been in God's presence. The moon is under her feet. Psalm 89 speaks of the steadfastness of God's covenant with David and says that it will be established like the moon, the faithful witness in the sky. [XCVI] She also has a victor's crown, not a king's crown, and it has 12 stars. All this beautiful imagery speaks eloquently of God's faithful people and his faithful covenant. Doesn't this draw you to her? Isn't she magnificent? This should draw us to faithfulness to God in Christ. This should encourage us to leave the futile life of sin and desire even more to be pleasing to the savior who bought us with his own blood.

The woman is a great sign, but the enormous, terrible red dragon is just another sign. This isn't just any old dragon, though. It has seven heads with seven royal crowns - not Victor's crowns - and ten horns. Seven and ten are numbers for completeness, right? So, this dragon is the representation of complete evil. It is red with the blood of the saints that it has martyred. The dragon is so big that its tail sweeps a third of the stars from the sky and flings them to the earth. Here is a clear sign that what we are reading is a vision, not something that will happen in reality. Even one star could not be flung to the Earth because stars are much bigger physically than the Earth is. Our sun, only a medium-sized star, is over 1.3 million times the size of the Earth, so there is no way one-third of the stars could land on the Earth. This is a sign of evil's rage personified by Satan and anyone he wishes to use to do his purpose of destroying God's people and creation. It is important to note that these two signs appear in heaven. We are being told about a spiritual battle that engulfs the entire history of time.

The woman is about to give birth, and the dragon is doing everything possible to ensure that the child doesn't survive.

Why is the dragon waiting for the child to be born? Why not just destroy the woman? Wouldn't that be easy enough? Clearly, this is not the case. The woman represents something that is beyond the dragon's ability to destroy. Either she is protected in some way by God, or she represents something that is beyond the dragon's power to take all at once – beyond the sweeping of stars from the sky, even. The woman, with the garments like the sun, standing on the moon – the faithful witness, the victor's crown of the followers of Christ, and the 12 stars – 12 representing the people of God, is a great sign of the faithful people of God in any age. There were 12 tribes of Israel and 12 apostles of the church. This is too big a problem for the dragon to attack, so he must focus on the child that will be born.

Repeatedly, Satan has tried to destroy God's plan. In the Garden of Eden, Satan used a serpent to deceive Eve. God was enjoying fellowship with His created family, Adam and Eve. Satan wanted to destroy that relationship, so he deceived Eve into sin, which he knew would hinder that relationship. What Satan didn't know is that God foreknew what Satan and Adam and Eve would do and had a plan. Satan acted in line with it in his attempt to thwart God's plan because God wants people to choose a relationship with Him as if it were their own idea. What we see here in Revelation is just what we are told about in Genesis 3 and summarized in verse 15, *And I will put enmity between you and the woman, and between your offspring and hers; he will crush your head, and you will strike his heel."*

Think of the many other examples in the Old Testament of how Satan tried to thwart God. Here are some examples: Cain killing Abel. The entire world is unfaithful to God, but there is Noah. Satan's attempts to tempt the aged Abraham and Sara before the birth of Isaac. How Satan tried to use Egypt to destroy Israel and Moses. Or how King Saul hunted David to kill him, whom God chose to be the (How many times?) great grandfather of Jesus. Remember, in 2 Kings 11, how Athaliah attempted to destroy the Messianic line? Or how in 2 Kings 20, Hezekiah, in the messianic line, almost died without an heir? Or how, in the book of Esther, Haman attempted to destroy all the Jews, but God had Esther in the right place at the right time? Or how Herod tried to kill Jesus? Or how Satan thought he won at the cross?

There is significance in that the woman wears a victor's crown, and the dragon wears a royal crown. The woman represents the people of God who are victorious because they follow the lamb. The dragon represents those who seem to rule the world, but they cannot defeat the people of God. The church is not overcome by the gates of hell.

The child is born. A son. A male child. One who will rule all nations with an iron scepter. You really must, at this point, read Psalm 2. Verse 9, speaking of God's son, says, "*You will break them with a rod of iron; you will dash them to pieces like pottery.*" However, you need to read the whole Psalm for the beautiful context. The child seems to be the Messiah, the son of God, Jesus. After he went to the cross, died for our sins, was buried, and was raised again on the third day, he ascended into heaven 40 days later. He was "snatched" up into heaven to God and to His throne. But it would seem to be even bigger than that. Those who have been baptized into Christ and have clothed themselves with Christ are also said to be reigning with him in heaven, even as we are still living on earth. [XCVII]

The woman of this great sign flees from the dragon to a place in the wilderness. Here, she will stay, provided for by God, for a brief time. We see the same 1260 days as the trampling of the city and the preaching of the two witnesses. We will elaborate more on this in verses 13-17, but let's pause and consider who this woman is and who the male child is. One of the reasons this is a great sign is that there are two different meanings. The woman is Mary giving birth to Jesus. She is also God's spiritual Israel in any period of time, past, present or future. Her children are Christians who keep God's commands and hold fast their testimony about Jesus.

MICHAEL AND HIS ANGELS

12:7, Then war broke out in heaven. Michael and his angels fought against the dragon, and the dragon and his angels fought back. 8, But he was not strong enough, and they lost their place in heaven. 9, The great dragon was hurled down—that ancient serpent called the devil, or Satan, who leads the whole world astray. He was hurled to the earth, and his angels with him.

The dragon has failed to devour the son of the woman, and to distract him from going after the woman, Michael declares war on the dragon. Michael is an angel of God who oversees other angels. There is a war in heaven between Michael and his angels and the dragon and his angels while the woman flees to a place in the wilderness on Earth. She had been a sign in heaven, but now she is a sign on earth.

Who is this, Michael? His name means, "who is like God?" (Google it!) Jude calls him an archangel.[XCVIII] In Daniel, [XCIX] he is called a chief prince and the great prince. In Daniel, we see Michael representing God in a conflict that the saints of God are experiencing. This is also what we see in this vision in Revelation.

Who is this dragon? He is an ancient serpent. In the most ancient time on earth, a serpent in the Garden of Eden deceived Eve.[C] This serpent is called the devil, which means "slanderer," and Satan, which means "adversary." He is the deceiver. In his name, we see the craft he used to bring sin into the world. Using his adversarial nature, he slandered God and deceived Eve into the sin that Adam participated in for the purpose that the devil could now slander Adam and Eve to God. What an evil being.

However, the dragon, Satan, was not powerful enough to defeat Michael and his angels. He lost his place in heaven, so he could no longer slander God's people to God's face. He is hurled to the earth with his angels, just like the stars that he swept from the sky. But that doesn't keep him from keeping up his adversarial, slanderous, deceiving ways. No, he goes about to lead the whole world astray. Destruction is his one purpose and intent. Why would I give his desires the time of day in my heart? All he wants to do is destroy me. Let's choose not to listen to his temptations. His slander. His deceit. After all, who has he defeated? He couldn't defeat a pregnant woman! He couldn't defeat an infant! He couldn't defeat God's messenger, Michael! [CI] Satan is defeated!

But how could salvation have come (12:10) when Satan is running free on earth to deceive people?

GOD'S VICTORY AND SATAN'S RESPONSE

12:10, Then I heard a loud voice in heaven say:

> *"Now have come the salvation and the power*
> *and the kingdom of our God,*
> *and the authority of his Messiah.*
> *For the accuser of our brothers and sisters,*
> *who accuses them before our God day and night,*
> *has been hurled down.*
> *11, They triumphed over him*
> *by the blood of the Lamb*
> *and by the word of their testimony;*
> *they did not love their lives so much*
> *as to shrink from death.*
> *12, Therefore rejoice, you heavens*
> *and you who dwell in them!*
> *But woe to the earth and the sea,*
> *because the devil has gone down to you!*
> *He is filled with fury,*
> *because he knows that his time is short."*

Now that Satan has been cast down. More than that hurled down, we see that four things have come.

1. The salvation of our God.

2. The power of our God.

3. The kingdom of our God.

4. The authority of His Messiah.

But when did this happen? Didn't God always have power? Hasn't He always been king? Hasn't He always been able to save? Yes, but now these things have been revealed powerfully to the world. I suggest that this happened during the 33 years of Jesus' life on earth, culminating in his death, burial, resurrection, and ascension into heaven. The ascension put a bow on the whole affair because it gives us the picture and hope that we may one day ascend with Christ and be with God for eternity. I only say "may" because it depends on God's saving power and our obedience to the gospel. [CII] That should make anyone ask the question, "How can one be obedient to the gospel?" I pray you ask that question and find the answer in the pages of God's word. John says that we may know that we have eternal life. [CIII] Look at all the things we "know" according to 1st John. In every case, obedience to the gospel is required. But the point is that you can know you are saved.

We saw above that the devil, Satan, is a slanderer and adversary, and now we also see that he has been our accuser. But now, he has been cast out of God's presence and can no longer do these things before God. He has been replaced in heaven with our mediator, one who has our salvation, not our demise, at heart. This one, Jesus, the Christ, stands before the Father. But there is woe on the earth because that is where Satan still has some freedom to roam. He still can slander and accuse me of my earthly self and, therefore, be my adversary.

Those who defeated Satan did so with some unusual weapons; there are only three of them.

1. The blood of the lamb.

2. The word of their testimony.

3. Love of Christ over love of life.

Because Satan is defeated, the heavens and those who reside there are told to rejoice. That's us, isn't it? Aren't Christians residing in heaven spiritually, even as we are living on earth physically? But those who are not Christians reside on earth both physically and spiritually. They have woe. But we hold out hope to them that they too can share in the rejoicing of having their sins washed away in the blood of the lamb, putting their hope in Christ and thus having a mediator standing before the face of God on their behalf. Who wouldn't want Jesus standing before God, saying about you, "This is my brother. He has no sins because I washed them away in my blood. Give him your protection and favor."

SATAN'S ATTACK CONTINUES

Satan is filled with fury on the earth because he knows that his time is short.

12:13, When the dragon saw that he had been hurled to the earth, he pursued the woman who had given birth to the male child. 14, The woman was given the two wings of a great eagle so that she might fly to the place prepared for her in the wilderness, where she would be taken care of for a time, times and half a time, out of the serpent's reach. 15 Then, from his mouth, the serpent spewed water like a river to overtake the woman and sweep her away with the torrent. 16, But the earth helped the woman by opening its mouth and swallowing the river that the dragon had spewed out of his mouth. 17, Then the dragon was enraged at the woman and went off to wage war against the rest of her offspring—those who keep God's commands and hold fast their testimony about Jesus.

Is there an event in the Old Testament that this part of the vision reminds you of? Satan tried to destroy the Israelite children as they were slaves in Egypt by commanding through

Pharaoh that all the baby boys should be drowned in the Nile River. Moses, a male child, was spared, however, and grew up with the knowledge of his heritage. Satan tried again to destroy him when he was forty years old and again failed. He continued his attack on the Israelites through Egypt until God gave them wings to fly away through 10 plagues, the last of which killed all the first-born Egyptians as well as their first-born animals. As they fled, they were led to be hemmed in by the Red Sea and the mountains while the Egyptians closed in behind them. Figuratively, Satan spewed water like a river to overtake Israel, the woman, but God caused a dry path for Israel to take to the safety of the wilderness. Read all about it in Exodus 1-15. God nourished and protected Israel for forty years in the wilderness before they entered the promised land.

We saw in verse 6 that the woman fled to the wilderness, where she would be cared for 1,260 days. This is a place prepared for her by God. Now, we see in verse 14 a little more detail. She was given two wings like a great eagle, which enabled her to fly to her prepared place. Here, the timeframe is a time, times, and half a time. 1260 days work out to be 3.5 years, or a time, times, and half a time. The point again is that it is a short, undefined duration. More important is the motif of the Eagle's wings. God says, in Exodus 19:4, about the Exodus, *"You yourselves have seen what I did to Egypt, and how I carried you on eagles' wings and brought you to myself."* The eagle's wings signify God's protecting work for his people.

Satan has been unable to defeat the pregnant woman; he was not able to devour her male child, and he could not get to her in the wilderness, so now he goes off to make war on the rest of her children. These are the ones who keep God's commands and hold fast to their testimony about Jesus. It seems that the woman represents spiritual Israel, whom Satan cannot collectively defeat. So, he goes off to war against individuals he can separate from the collective (please note the Star Trek Next Generation reference). Satan's only chance is to get us alone. We must not miss the point that whether the righteous live or die, they are exempt from judgment. Jim McGuiggan, in his wonderful book on Revelation, [civ] devotes over four pages to verse 11. I encourage you to purchase that book if you only want to read those four pages.

As we move on to Revelation chapter 13, we'll see that the Dragon isn't finished just yet. Now, he brings reinforcements! But do not be worried; do not be dismayed; God can still save you. Keep your faith in Jesus, follow Him, walk in His light, and you will find your way safely through whatever Satan tries to throw at you.

CHAPTER 9

THE TWO BEASTS

Revelation 13:1 to 13:18.

The dragon has failed in his purpose in every attempt. He and his angels were unsuccessful in everything they tried to do to stop God's purpose from succeeding. But the dragon only has one purpose: to oppose God. Now, Satan, in the form of the dragon, brings reinforcements: a beast from the sea and a beast from the land. It will be interesting to see how Satan tries to use God's methods for his purpose. Will he succeed this time?

THE FIRST BEAST

13:1, The dragon stood on the shore of the sea. And I saw a beast coming out of the sea. It had ten horns and seven heads, with ten crowns on its horns, and on each head, a blasphemous name. 2, The beast I saw resembled a leopard but had feet like those of a bear and a mouth like that of a lion. The dragon gave the beast his power, throne, and great authority. 3, One of the heads of the beast seemed to have had a fatal wound, but the fatal wound had been healed. The whole world was filled with wonder and followed the beast. 4, People worshiped the dragon because he had given authority to the beast, and they also worshiped the beast and asked, "Who is like the beast? Who can wage war against it?"

5, The beast was given a mouth to utter proud words and blasphemies and to exercise its authority for forty-two months. 6, It opened its mouth to blaspheme God and to slander his name and his dwelling place and those who live in heaven. 7, It was given power to wage war against God's holy people and to conquer them. And it was given authority over every tribe, people, language, and nation. 8, All inhabitants of the earth will worship the beast—all whose names have not been written in the Lamb's book of life, the Lamb who was slain from the creation of the world. 9, Whoever has ears, let them hear. 10, "If anyone is to go into captivity, into captivity they will go. If anyone is to be killed with the sword, with the sword, they will be killed." This calls for patient endurance and faithfulness on the part of God's people.

Table 8: Vision Comparison

Daniel 2:31-45	Daniel 7:1-14	Revelation 13:1-10	Interpretation
Large Statue	**Four beasts out of the sea**	**Sea Beast**	
Head of Pure Gold	Lion	Mouth of a lion	Babylon
Chest & arms of silver	Bear	Feet of a bear	Media & Persia
Belly & thighs of bronze	Leopard	Resembled a leopard	Greece
Legs of iron, feet of mixed iron & clay	Terrifying Beast with 10 horns	10 horns	Rome
Feet attacked, and the whole statue falls	The last beast is slain, and the other 3 disappear with it	Sea beast has the characteristics of three beasts of Daniel	

The dragon stands by the sea, and a beast emerges from the water. You might say the beast is at the dragon's beck and call. Check out these two references to the sea. First from Isaiah, *But the wicked are like the tossing sea, which cannot rest, whose waves cast up mire and mud.* [CV] And from

Revelation, *Then the angel said to me, "The waters you saw, where the prostitute sits, are peoples, multitudes, nations, and languages.*[CVI] Therefore, from the local context as well as the context of scripture, the beast from the sea seems to represent the restless movements and instability of the nations and people of the earth. Now, as we have seen when we refer to "people of the earth," we are referring to those who do not belong to the Lord.

The sea beast had 10 horns and a royal crown on each horn. These are royal crowns worn by those who presume to be kings on earth, not the victor's crowns worn by those who follow Christ. We see then that the sea beast is the current governing authority. At the time of John's writing, that was, of course, Rome. The 10 horns indicate great strength. Many people try to match up the 10 horns and crowns to the client kings of Rome or kings of Rome in some way. I believe that such details are unnecessary and confusing. The point is that those with power on earth are using their power in opposition to God's people and using it to persecute them.

The sea beast has seven heads, and according to Revelation 17:9, those seven heads are the seven hills upon which a prostitute sits. There are many theories about what these seven heads represent. Rome is said to sit on seven hills, so the fact that the seven heads are said to be seven hills makes the reference to Rome almost obvious. Other people suggest that at the time of the writing of Revelation, there were seven significant kings of Rome. My favorite theory is that the seven heads represent seven great empires. They are generally listed as Egypt, Assyria, Babylon, Medo-Persia, Greece, Rome, and some future empires. I like that the future empire could apply to any time in history since the fall of Rome. Again, none of these theories really matter! The fact is that each of the heads has a blasphemous name written on them. Regardless of what they specifically represent, they surely represent governments or groups of people who are in an adversarial relationship with

God. They blaspheme God. By their words and actions, they hate God.

Wow! All that from verse 1. In verse two, we see that the sea beast resembles three animals: A leopard's body, a bear's feet, and a lion's mouth. In Daniel 7, verses 4 through 6, we see beasts of these same animals in reverse order. A fourth beast is noted in Daniel 7:7, which is very terrifying and has 10 horns. A thorough study of Daniel shows these beasts to be Greece, Persia, Babylon, and Rome. The three animal representations of the beast of Revelation are in reverse order to Daniel's vision because John is looking back in time versus Daniel, who was looking forward through time.

The dragon gives the sea beast his power, throne, and great authority. Wait a minute, isn't the dragon Satan? Yes. Was not Satan unable to defeat God's messenger, a pregnant woman or even an infant? What power, throne, and authority did he have then? That's right. None. He can only look like he has these things because of what God allows him to exercise. But He's faking it. Speaking of faking it, the sea beast has a head that looks as if it had been fatally wounded but that it had been healed. So, he's also faking a death and resurrection like our Lord's. Don't fall for it. Don't be like the majority who are amazed by this false savior. No government can save you. There is only one. His name is Jesus. If you want true life, He's the only one who can give it to you. But this is a big deal. The beast resembles the dragon; as we'll soon see, the fatal wound draws people away from their true savior.

Those who are taken in amazement by the beast follow it and worship the dragon and the beast. They ask an interesting question. "Who is like the beast, and who is able to wage war with him?" A similar question was asked when the sixth seal was opened. There, these same people wanted to have the mountains and rocks fall on them to hide them from the wrath of the Lamb. They asked, "Who is able to stand?"[CVII] As we saw in the seventh chapter of Revelation, those who can stand are the ones who belong to Christ and are in Christ. They are the answer to the question, "Who is able to stand?" They also answer the question, "Who is able to wage war with him?" Those in Christ are not the ones who wage war against the beast. It is the Lamb that wages war against the beast. But they are in Christ; therefore, they are involved in the war that Christ is winning.

The first beast received great authority over four items, again pointing to his reign's earthly nature. He has authority over every tribe, every people, every language, and every nation. He has a mouth that utters proud words, and he blasphemes the God of heaven. And the people of the earth love it. They are astonished at the death and resurrection of the beast, so they follow the beast and worship it and the dragon that gave it power. Consider who is blasphemed by the beast. 1. God and His name, 2. God's dwelling place, and 3. Those who live in heaven – Christians. Three items, so we are talking about heavenly things. The beast makes war against those who live in heaven. Also known as "Christians" and "Saints." He is even able to conquer some of them.

Those who worship the beast are inhabitants of the earth. They are not Christians, and their names are not written in the Book of Life that belongs to the Lamb who had been slain from the creation of the world. They think they found their savior from the moral responsibilities the God of heaven laid on them. But he only gets to exercise his authority for 42 months. The same 42 months that the city is trampled over, the same 1260 days the two witnesses are prophesying, the same 1260 days that the woman is cared for in the desert, and the time, times, and half a time of her care. All these methods of relating transient time are of the same duration.

Let's quickly summarize the counterfeit nature of the beast. First, it is a counterfeit Christ, with its head showing signs of death, but it is alive. Second, it had counterfeit power. This power requires permission from God for the beast to be allowed to use it and from man to allow the beast to use it on them. Third, it was a counterfeit god as it enticed people to worship it, asking, "Who is like the beast? Who is able to wage war against it?" Fourth, it is a counterfeit government. Government is counterfeit when it is not used in line with God's will.

We have seen the persecution of the saints by the sea beast, and now, before we move on to the land beast, there is an admonition to the saints. In this unusual event, the KJV/NKJV translates this better, so here is Revelation 13:9-10 in the NKJV. *9, If anyone has an ear, let him hear. 10, He who leads into captivity shall go into captivity; he who kills with the sword must be killed with the sword. Here is the patience and the faith of the saints.* First, the ones who will hear are those who are listening to the Lord. Those who lead people into captivity and those who kill with the sword are those who persecute the saints. The saints must have faith and patience. Although they are being persecuted seemingly without limit, it is limited to the time frame represented by 42 months. Also, they must understand that their persecutors will get their persecutions turned back on their heads in the next life, if not this one.

THE SECOND BEAST

13:11, *Then I saw a second beast, coming out of the earth. It had two horns like a lamb, but it spoke like a dragon. 12, It exercised all the authority of the first beast on its behalf and made the earth and its inhabitants worship the first beast, whose fatal wound had been healed. 13, And it performed great signs, even causing fire to come down from heaven to the earth in full view of the people. 14, Because of the signs it was given the power to perform on behalf of the first beast, it deceived the inhabitants of the earth. It ordered them to set up an image in honor of the beast who was wounded by the sword and yet lived. 15, The second beast was given the power to give breath to the image of the first beast so that the image could speak and cause all who refused to worship the image to be killed. 16,*

It also forced all people, great and small, rich and poor, free and slave, to receive a mark on their right hands or on their foreheads, 17, so that they could not buy or sell unless they had the mark, which is the name of the beast or the number of its name.

18, This calls for wisdom. Let the person who has insight calculate the number of the beast, for it is the number of a man. That number is 666.

The second beast comes out of the earth, but the only thing we know about it as far as its appearance is that it has two horns like a lamb. That in itself is not very scary, but it speaks like a dragon. The earthly beast has no physical power, but that doesn't keep it from speaking as if it does. It exercised authority and performed miracles on behalf of the sea beast, so it had no authority or power to perform its own miracles. When it makes the earth and its inhabitants worship the first beast, it does so only through intimidation, deceiving them into believing the dragon and the two beasts have real power. It is all counterfeit. Yet he can still command people to set up an image in honor of the sea best. And they do it. This is where it gets tricky: how does the land beast with only counterfeit power give life to the image of the sea beast? Such a life that the image could kill all those who refused to worship it.

Later in Revelation,[CVIII] the second beast is called the false prophet. Many commentators spend significant time and energy finding meaning in these beasts and relating them to specific things on earth. One example is that the two horns represent the forces that created and enforced emperor worship. One horn represents the council who crafted images to facilitate emperor worship, and the other horn represents the prefects who enforced the worship. Another example is that the beast represents the false religion of the emperor cult or certain church groups with their religious apparatus that controls and exploits them. Maybe these things are so, but I'm saying that seeking specific examples is unnecessary. What we are seeing is the way Satan, the dragon, uses many avenues, including false religion, to deceive the people of the earth and draw them after him. We are being warned of his methods, and those who want a successful eternal life will do well to be careful not to be deceived.

We should also note that the beast was given the powers he employed. His actions and power were allowed by God, who has ultimate control over them. The land beast was counterfeit in three areas, signifying a counterfeit deity. First, he was like a lamb, so he was mimicking Christ. Second, he had counterfeit power, which was allowed only by God and man. Third, he did counterfeit miracles. Consider Acts 8:9-11 where Simon the Sorcerer deceives people with his fake miracles. When Philip showed up performing real miracles, he was amazed. However, until Philip showed up, Simon was able to amaze those around him. That is how the second beast deceived the people of the earth.

THE MARK OF THE BEAST

The people of the earth were forced to receive the mark of the beast. This is the mark of the land beast, not the dragon or the sea beast. Everyone, be they small or great, rich or poor, free or slave, had to receive the mark. The purpose of the mark was to allow for commerce to take place. I'm sure this comes about by deception as well. I can hear it saying, "Look, this will make everything easier for you. You'll know that the transaction you are making will work. All you need to do is have this mark on your right hand or your forehead. Then you'll be able to buy and sell without worry."

The mark is said to be the name of the beast or the number of his name. Then, it is said to be a man's number, or it could be translated as the number of a man. Man's number would mean that the number represents man in general, and the number of a man would mean one man specifically. Then, we are given the number six hundred and sixty-six, or 666.

This is one place in scripture where we are being told to calculate the name of the beast, seemingly representing a man since it is man's number. We're told that a wise person can calculate the name. Here are some examples of what people have come up with. First, emperor Domitian's full title was "Autokrator Kaisar Dometianus Germanicus," which, using the numerical values of the letters, calculates to 666. Also, the title "Vicarius Filii Dei" used by some popes equates to 666. Finally, "Nero Caesar," translated into Hebrew, is Neron Kaiser, which is calculated to be 666. Are all these different representations of the beast?

Perhaps we see the number 6, representing less than perfect, being repeated three times for emphasis. We've noted before that three attributes are used to designate a deity, so this could represent a counterfeit deity. God is spoken of as Holy, Holy, Holy, and in the last three trumpets, we had Woe, Woe, Woe, emphasizing the terror to come upon the earth and the people thereof. Also, if the number 6 is corrupt and counterfeit compared to 7, then one 6 could be assigned to each beast: The dragon, the sea beast, and the land beast. Also, as we've noticed before, all of Satan's efforts to thwart God's plans end in abject failure. So, we see failure (6) upon failure (6) upon failure (6).

Search this on the internet, and you'll find no end to the views and calculations for the number 666. Here is the important takeaway. We have seen two groups of people receive a mark. One group gets the Mark of Christ; the other group gets the Mark of the Beast. Everyone has a mark. If you don't have the Mark of Christ, you will have the Mark of the Beast. The Mark of Christ keeps those who own it alive, and all others die. The Mark of the Beast keeps those who own it alive, and all others die. How can both be true? The Mark of Christ relates to spiritual life and spiritual death. The Mark of the Beast relates to physical life and physical death. The one who has the Mark of Christ will be kept alive spiritually even if they die physically. The one who has the Mark of the Beast will be kept alive physically for a time but is dead spiritually.

Wisdom exists in having the Mark of Christ and being kept alive spiritually because, through that blessing, you will obtain eternal life.

CHAPTER 10

THE SEVEN VOICES

Revelation 14:1 to 14:20.

After seeing the dragon's fury, the sea beast's power, and the land beast's deception, a Christian might wonder how there is any hope for them.

THE FIRST VOICE

14:1, Then I looked, and there before me was the Lamb, standing on Mount Zion, and with him 144,000 who had his name and his Father's name written on their foreheads. 2, And I heard a sound from heaven like the roar of rushing waters and like a loud peal of thunder. The sound I heard was like that of harpists playing their harps. 3, And they sang a new song before the throne and before the four living creatures and the elders. No one could learn the song except the 144,000 who had been redeemed from the earth. 4, These are those who did not defile themselves with women, for they remained virgins. They follow the Lamb wherever he goes. They were purchased from among mankind and offered as first fruits to God and the Lamb. 5, No lie was found in their mouths; they are blameless.

Let's do a little review. Satan, appearing as a red dragon, stalked a pregnant woman so he could devour her male baby as soon as he was born. He failed and ended up facing the angel Michael in battle. He lost that battle and was thrown down to the earth, where he persecuted the woman and attempted to kill her. He failed again, so he went to war with the rest of her children. For this purpose, he enlists the help of the beast from the sea and the beast from the earth. The intention of the three beasts (Dragon, Sea, Earth) is to destroy those who have the mark of Christ and make them take up the mark of the beast. But those who have the mark of Christ overcame him because of the blood of the Lamb and because of the word of their testimony, and they did not love their life even when faced with death. For this reason, rejoice, you heavens and you who dwell in them.[CIX]

Revelation chapter 14 starts with John saying, "Then I looked." You would think he would have stopped looking by now! But I'm glad he is still looking. He sees The Lamb, not that counterfeit one that came up out of the earth. This one is Standing on Mount Zion. This is the same lamb that earlier looked as if it had been slain, but he is now standing powerfully, resolutely, victoriously on Mount Zion. Look at Psalm 2. Doesn't this beautifully summarize what we're seeing in Revelation? Mount Zion is God's holy mountain[CX] and the place from which God's salvation emanated.[CXI]

The Lamb stands with the 144,000 we saw earlier in Chapter 7 of Revelation. Let's look at how they are described here in chapter 14.

Table 9: The Description of the 144,000

- The Lamb's name and the Father's name are on their foreheads.
- They are with the Lamb on Mount Zion (on earth).
- They sang a new song.
- They stood before the throne (in heaven), the four creatures, and the 24 elders.
- They were the only ones who could learn the song.
- They had been redeemed from the earth.
- They were male virgins.
- They follow the Lamb wherever he goes.
- They were purchased from among men and offered as first fruits to God and the lamb.
- No lie was found in their mouths.
- They are blameless.

Now, remember the description of the 144,000 from Revelation 7.

- They were on earth.
- They are sealed on the forehead.
- They are from all the tribes of Israel.
- 12,000 come from each tribe listed.

If we take the 144,000 literally, we must take some other things literally, as in the following list.

- They were simultaneously standing on Mount Zion on Earth AND before the throne in heaven.
- No women are included.
- No Elders or Deacons are included since they are required to be married.
- There must be exactly 12,000 from each tribe listed, and only those tribes.
- They have never lied.
- The seal and names written on their foreheads must literally be there.

- The person who started the Jehovah's Witnesses is not included since he was married and divorced. But then he didn't belong to one of the 12 tribes of Israel, either.

If this passage is to be taken figuratively, as seems necessary, then what is the alternative? How do we understand the list of 144,000? First, it seems apparent that 144,000 only represents the complete number. In Jewish numerology, 12 represents the people of God, and 1000 represents a large, undefined number. Then, 12 x 12 x 1000 represents the complete number of God's redeemed people. In other words, no one is missing. The 144,000 have the name and seal on their forehead, which indicates that God's character is exemplified in their lives. The unbelievers have the mark of the beast, and their lives mirror their master. They sang the song of the redeemed, which only the redeemed can learn because it comes from the character of the one in whom they have put their trust. They are physically on earth, but spiritually, they are in heaven. They have not given in to idolatry, so they are counted as virgins. They have called only Jesus, Lord. In many ways, in travel and in business, one had to affirm that "Caesar is Lord." A faithful Christian would not do this, so there was no lie on their lips.

In the Old Testament, idolatry was often referred to as adultery. Therefore, those in this group are called virgins because they have been married to God and have refused to defile that relationship by associating with other gods. They are also called the first fruits. The first fruits were offered to God. They testified to the fact that the harvest all belonged to God and that more would follow.[CXII] The fact that the 144,000 are the first fruits would add weight to the position that the 144,000 are those on earth who are exalting over the conquest of the beast instead of the final exaltation since the fact that they are the first fruit would suggest there would be more to follow.

THE VOICES OF TWO ANGELS

The second and third Voices

14:6, Then I saw another angel flying in midair, and he had the eternal gospel to proclaim to those who live on the earth— to every nation, tribe, language, and people. 7 He said in a loud voice, "Fear God and give him glory because the hour of his judgment has come. Worship him who made the heavens, the earth, the sea, and the springs of water." 8, A second angel followed and said, "'Fallen! Fallen is Babylon the Great,' which made all the nations drink the maddening wine of her adulteries." 9, A third angel followed them...

Now, John sees three angels flying in the air, one after the other. Again, it is important to note that this is a vision. The first angel has the eternal gospel. We know that the gospel is the good news of the opportunity to find salvation in the power of Jesus' death, burial, and resurrection, as Paul told us in 1 Corinthians 15:1-4. We have also been informed of the eternal nature of this gospel in Ephesians 1. In Ephesians 1:3, we are told that before creation, God chose to make us holy and blameless by being in Christ. 1 Peter 1:17-19 informs us that Christ was chosen before the creation of the world as the lamb without blemish or defect, whose blood would redeem us from the empty way of life handed down to us by our parents. The gospel is then completed for each individual when Romans 6, especially verses 1-7, makes clear that it is through baptism that we die to sin as Jesus died on the cross and that we are raised in Christ to live a new and holy life. Nothing could be more wonderfully simple than that!

This wonderful, eternal gospel is to be preached to four groups of people, and we see again how John keeps the pattern of his writing consistent. The whole of creation is described by four attributes: every nation, tribe, language, and people. The angel now says in a loud voice, our second of seven voices, that the whole of creation should do three things in relation to God.

So again, we see three attributes in relation to God: Fear Him, Give Him Glory, and Worship Him. We are to worship him who created, and what he created is described by four attributes: the heavens, the earth, the sea, and the springs of water. John is consistent in his use of numerology. All creation should glorify the eternal God who made all creation. God alone is worthy of worship. All else has been created by him and is therefore inferior to him.

In the gospel, we see the defeat of Satan. We are told to fear God, give him glory, and worship him because the hour of his judgment on Satan and those he uses has come. As Jim McGuiggan states in his book on Revelation,[CXIII] "God alone is worthy of worship, and the coming events will prove that clearly. Now, this good news is good news indeed. It doesn't matter in what age the Devil is manifesting himself - he is USING the nations. He deceives them and blinds them. His defeat is good news!"

Now, the second angel declares that Babylon the Great has fallen. We've noted in a previous chapter how similar the description of the great city in Revelation is to the fourth kingdom in Daniel's prophecy. Babylon, which was the great city of Daniel's day, had fallen. If Revelation is using Babylon to refer to Rome, why is the fall of Rome spoken of in the past tense? Simply put, it emphasizes the surety of the fulfillment of the prophecy. See Paul's explanation of God's use of the past tense in Romans 4:16-17. Here, Paul says that God told Abraham that he "made" (past tense) Abraham a father of many nations.[CXIV] At the time that God told this to Abraham, Abraham had only one descendant. God is teaching us something particularly important here about life and how our brains work, which is what the success industry and Vince Poscente, in his book, *The Ant and the Elephant*, have picked up on. Let me use Vince's words through his character, Brio,[CXV] "If you keep your focus on the want, you'll probably get nothing but a continued experience of wanting. Focus on having something, and you'll eventually get it." God frames things that are to come as if they have already happened. We must see our desired future as something that has already happened. We are created in God's image, so we have similar powers that He has, just not to the level he has them. If you are in Christ, then you have His Holy Spirit working in you as well, so if your desired future is in line with God's desires for you, then you should see that future as sure, as fulfilled, or as Alanis Morissette put it "as sure as rain on your wedding day, or a free ride when you've already paid, don't you think?"[CXVI]

Babylon had "made all nations drink the wine of the passion of her sexual immorality." Just as Babylon had been the commerce center of the world and to do business in the world, you had to do it through Babylon, so before them was Nineveh, and at the time of Revelation, it was Rome. Rome, however, took their oppression regarding commerce to a new level. The reference here is to commerce because, as we saw previously,[CXVII] no one could buy or sell without the mark of the beast. In many places, to do business, you had to offer incense and worship to the emperor. You had to drink the wine of the passion of her sexual immorality. Often in the Old Testament, offering worship to anyone but God was portrayed as sexual immorality. For many years now, the only way to do business in the world has been through the U.S. dollar. The U.S. has been the center of commerce for the world. Is it becoming the new Babylon? If so, what do we do about it before God's judgment comes upon this nation? We do what Christians have always done. Share the gospel with one person at a time. Help them join the ranks of the 144,000 who were considered virgins because they did not drink Babylon's wine. Give them eternal hope, not hope based on short-term devotion to whatever financial system has the power at the moment. One thing for sure is that God will not let oppression continue forever.

THE VOICE OF THE THIRD ANGEL

The fourth and fifth Voices

14:9, A third angel followed them and said in a loud voice: "If anyone worships the beast and its image and receives its mark on their forehead or on their hand, 10, They, too, will drink the wine of God's fury, which has been poured full strength into the cup of his wrath. They will be tormented with burning sulfur in the presence of the holy angels and of the Lamb. 11, And the smoke of their torment will rise forever and ever. There will be no rest day or night for those who worship the beast and its image, or for anyone who receives the mark of its name." 12, This calls for patient endurance on the part of the people of God who keep his commands and remain faithful to Jesus. 13, Then I heard a voice from heaven say, "Write this: Blessed are the dead who die in the Lord from now on." "Yes," says the Spirit, "they will rest from their labor, for their deeds will follow them."

The third angel has a lot to say. The second angel called out wrath on Babylon because she *made* all the nations drink her wine. It is clear by what the third angel says that those who drank her wine had the choice to do so. To not drink her wine may have seemed like physical suicide, but to do so is spiritual suicide, as the third angel says, as we have seen previously in our study. "If" anyone worships the beast and his image – that is why he receives the mark of the beast on his forehead or right hand. This person got drunk on Babylon's wine, but he isn't done drinking! Now, he gets to drink the wine of God's wrath, too. The wine of God's wrath is mixed with full strength in the cup of his anger. Wow. Maybe, just maybe, it would make sense for me to turn from evil and turn my life over to the God who has the power to destroy Babylon and all who worship her. Why would I worship a false god that has no power over the real one? Why would I let the temporary pressure of this world keep me from the eternal glory that I could have with the true and living God?

How does the judgment on those who worship the beast make you feel? They will be tormented with burning sulfur in the presence of God's holy angels and the Lamb. The smoke of their torment will rise forever and ever. They will have no rest ever, day or night. This seems like a terrible existence, beyond understanding, for those so judged. It doesn't seem like a very desirable existence for the angels attending to the judgment or the Lamb either. What is going on here? We must not forget that we are experiencing a vision – look ahead in this chapter and see how the son of man harvests the earth with a sharp sickle (verse 16). He's not harvesting wheat – he's harvesting people – not something you do with a sharp sickle. The point here is that you do not want the results of worshiping the beast – in the end, those results are horrible. It is eternal death. Back to the question I asked about how this judgment makes you feel. That is the whole point of Revelation. All the things we need to avoid and run from are depicted as extremely devastating and full of turmoil. All the things we need to enjoy and run to are depicted as extremely beautiful and peaceful. This puts in our hearts the motivation to seek the Lord while he may be found. To walk in his ways while we have life to do so. The night is coming when no man can work, so let's do the will of him who saved us while it is day.

As verse 12 says, "This calls for patient endurance on the part of the people of God who keep his commands and remain faithful to Jesus." Look, those who worship the beast may have an easy time of it now as they have all the support they need to keep living their evil ways as they are fed by the beast and kept physically alive by him. But their end is destruction. So, patiently endure the difficulties you have in life as you keep God's commandments and remain faithful to Jesus. In the end, you will be so glad you did. This leads us to the voice from heaven, "Blessed are the dead who die in the Lord from now on." In the introductory chapter, we discussed that there are seven blessings in the book of Revelation. The first is in chapter 1, verse 3, and the second blessing is here in chapter 14, verse

13. Blessed are those who die in the Lord. God knows those who are his and will keep them spiritually safe and blessed for eternity. They are blessed because they will rest from their labor. The labor was partly due to resisting the great temptation to give in to the beast and all the false pleasure and security he had to offer. Take a moment and review the parable of the rich man and Lazarus in Luke 16:19-31. Notice that in the scene after Lazarus and the rich man had died, all the dialogue and activity is between Moses and the rich man. Lazarus is at rest, and Abraham protects that rest. Consider the difference in the view of death held by those who are unfaithful compared to those who are faithful. The unfaithful have every reason to fear death; it will be torment, even if it is just that they will not ever have rest. The faithful have every reason to look forward to death because they will have rest and get to enjoy the glory of their Lord.

THE HARVEST OF THE EARTH

The Sixth Voice

14:14, I looked, and there before me was a white cloud, and seated on the cloud was one like a son of man with a crown of gold on his head and a sharp sickle in his hand. 15, Then another angel came out of the temple and called in a loud voice to him who was sitting on the cloud, "Take your sickle and reap because the time to reap has come, for the harvest of the earth is ripe." 16, So he who was seated on the cloud swung his sickle over the earth, and the earth was harvested.

This is interesting. John sees one like a son of man, Jesus, the Christ, sitting on a cloud, and an angel tells him what to do. This angel came out of the temple and called out in a loud voice – notice that all these angel voices are loud – that the one on the cloud should reap the earth. John sees an angel telling the Son of God to put in his sickle and reap because the harvest of the earth is ripe. How is it that an angel gets to tell Jesus what to do? This angel came out of the temple where God the Father is, as we can see in the picture of the throne room in Revelation 8:3-5. There, we saw that God faced the altar where the prayers of the saints were an offering before him made by fire with incense. The angel is simply relaying a message from the Father to the Son that the time for reaping has come. Remember that Jesus said, as recorded in Matthew 24:36, that He nor the angels knew when the day of judgment would be and that only the Father knew that. Upon receiving the message, the Son simply sets the judgment in motion, and the righteous are gathered up for their reward like wheat is gathered into a barn.

We have seen Jesus in his glory on the Isle of Patmos on earth,[CXVIII] as a Lamb in heaven standing between the throne of God and the 24 elders,[CXIX] as the Lamb at the center of the throne,[CXX] as the Lamb standing on Mount Zion on earth,[CXXI] and now we see him as one like a son of man on a white cloud. This must be about his return to earth when he takes the saints home since that is exactly what he does here: He swings his sharp sickle and harvests the good grapes.

Remember how we were told earlier[CXXII] that there would be no more delays? What have we seen since then? Just an introduction to all the chess pieces in the cosmic battle between good and evil that is about to be joined. The stage is set. The chess pieces are taking their positions. Whose side are you joining? Choose wisely.

THE SEVENTH VOICE

14:17, Another angel came out of the temple in heaven, and he, too, had a sharp sickle. 18, Still another angel, who had charge of the fire, came from the altar and called in a loud voice to him who had the sharp sickle, "Take your sharp sickle and gather the clusters of grapes from the earth's vine because its grapes are ripe." 19, The angel swung his sickle on the earth, gathered its grapes, and threw them into the great winepress of God's wrath. 20, They were trampled in the winepress outside the city, and blood flowed out of the press, rising as high as the horses' bridles for a distance of 1,600 stadia.

John sees, in his vision, another angel coming out of the temple and still another angel coming from the altar. So here, a second angel comes from God, and an angel comes from the altar, representing the prayers of the saints. The angel coming from God has a sharp sickle, and the angel representing the will of the saints speaks our seventh voice. Essentially, the saints tell God's servant that it's time for judgment. Remember, in Revelation 6:9-11, we saw the martyrs ask God how long until their blood would be avenged. They were told to rest a little while longer. It appears that their request for justice is about to be carried out. It is pictured as the prayers of the saints commanding the angel of God, but it is a picture of God, in his perfect timing, responding to the prayers of the saints.

Notice that, in verse 16, Jesus harvested Christians from over the earth, but the angel harvests the unrighteous from on the earth, verse 19. Christians live above the earth. As we have said, Christians live in heaven even while they reside on the earth. But those who are not in Christ live and reside on the earth. Jesus takes and protects those who are his, but the rest – the grapes of wrath – are unprotected and are trampled in the great winepress of God's wrath.

This great winepress of God's wrath is "outside the city." This is an interesting turn of phrase. Where was Jesus crucified? Outside the city. This was a sign of reproach against Jesus[CXXIII] that his followers also bore. But now, those who were reproachful of Jesus and his followers, those who trampled the holy city,[CXXIV] would share Jesus' reproach and be trampled outside the city.

The blood coming out from the wine press was the depth of a horse's bridle, and it ran for a distance of 1600 stadia, something like 184 miles or 296 km. C'mon. This is a vision; this is not literal. The point of this is to evoke a very severe emotional reaction. Can you think of a devastation that is more colossal, more gut-wrenching, more vomit-inducing than that? If you think about this from a numerology standpoint, 1600 stadia is 4 x 4 x 10 x 10, equaling the complete (10 x 10) judgment of the people of the earth (4 x 4).

Do you need more motivation to turn away from wickedness and give your life over to the love and protection of the Son of God? What would keep you from choosing obedience to the one who has your life in his hands? Give your heart fully to him. Don't hold anything back. He will bring you safely through to peace, love, and glory.

CHAPTER 11

THE SEVEN BOWLS

Revelation 15:1 to 16:21.

There were the seven seals that, when opened, revealed God's judgment. Then there were the seven trumpets that, when blown, announced God's judgment. Now, there are seven bowls that, when poured out, bring God's judgment. There was a chance to repent when God's judgment was revealed and when it was announced. Will there be a chance to repent when God's judgment is poured out?

PREFACE TO THE SEVEN BOWLS

15:1, I saw in heaven another great and marvelous sign: seven angels with the seven last plagues—last because with them God's wrath is completed. 2, And I saw what looked like a sea of glass glowing with fire and, standing beside the sea, those who had been victorious over the beast and its image and over the number of its name. They held harps given them by God. 3, and sang the song of God's servant Moses and of the Lamb:

> *"Great and marvelous are your deeds,*
> *Lord God Almighty.*
> *Just and true are your ways,*
> *King of the nations.*
> *4, Who will not fear you, Lord,*
> *and bring glory to your name?*
> *For you alone are holy.*
> *All nations will come*
> *and worship before you,*
> *for your righteous acts have been revealed."*

John sees in heaven a great and marvelous sign. A little earlier, he saw a woman clothed with the sun,[CXXV] and he called that vision a great sign. This sign even eclipses that one as it is great *and* marvelous. He sees seven angels with the seven *last* plagues. As is so often true in Revelation, John explains what he means by the *last plagues*. In the process of pouring out these plagues, God's judgment is complete; *it is finished*.

Let's take another foray into the question: why isn't Revelation written literally rather than with all these signs and symbols? As you know by now, I believe that God is using our created emotional makeup to motivate us away from evil and toward righteousness through imagery. There are many examples of God using imagery in His word. Read Isaiah 13, where God forecasts the coming judgment on Babylon by use of the Medes. Complete destruction is symbolized but not actually carried out. Remember, Daniel was living in the capital city of Babylon when it was overtaken by the Medes, but he survived to serve the Medes. This event isn't much more than a footnote in Daniel's story.[CXXVI] Read through the Old Testament, and you'll see that it isn't unusual for God to use signs and symbols. But why does God choose to speak this way? If we understand that Revelation refers to Rome, the figurehead of the persecution of Christians, then we must understand that Rome, like Babylon, would not fall completely but would never rule the world again. Consider that God wants our emotions involved, and that can best happen using signs and symbols that are colossal. Also, consider that God probably does not want us to limit the message to Rome only. What if we need to see this as referring to any country or city that would become Babylon or Rome-like?

ANGELS AND VICTORS

Where did the victors stand? They are standing beside (or on) a sea of glass. Think back again to Revelation 4:6, where we first saw the sea of glass standing before the throne. This again indicates the difference between God's kingdom and the kingdoms of men. God's kingdom is represented by a sea of gentle, still waters, whereas the kingdoms of men are represented by turbulent, deadly waters. Those who are victorious over the temptations of the beast are given the ability to stand safely on the sea of glass – to walk on water. Those standing on the sea of glass are those who were victorious over the beast and his image and the number of his name. They are the 144,000 spoken of in chapters 14 and 7. They have the seal and God's name on their foreheads. Now, think back to the Old Testament and see the parallel of this vision to the priests of Israel. See in 2 Chronicles 4:4-6 how Solomon made a sea for the priests to wash in. Now we see those who have washed their robes and made them white in the blood of the lamb, [CXXVII] standing on the sea. The Old Testament priests had a seal on their foreheads: "HOLY TO THE LORD," [CXXVIII] as these standing on the sea of glass have the sign of God.

Notice that the sea of glass looked like it was mixed with fire. How awesome and awe-inspiring that must have been to see. Is the fire representing the glory of God like a consuming fire,[CXXIX] or is the fire burning the dross of our sin to make us holy,[CXXX] or is it God's judgment or the trials we must go through to be close to God? Perhaps "yes" to all of the above.

The victors standing on the sea of glass are holding harps that had been given to them by God, and they sang a song. This is just more detail being added to what we read in Revelation 14:2- 3 - ...*The sound I heard was like that of harpists playing their harps. 3 And they sang a new song...* The harps are a visible, physical representation of the melodious voices of the victors singing the song that only they could learn because they were victorious. People who aren't successful in their battle against the temptations of Satan can't learn the song. It's the song of Moses, the victor in the Old Testament, and the Lamb, the victor in the New Testament and for all time. In Exodus 15, we hear Moses' song of victory when God saved them through the waters of the Red Sea from the Egyptian hordes. It is the song of the Lamb, the one responsible for all the victories of the saints, from Moses on and before.

What song are they singing? It is a song of praise to the God of gods, the King of kings. His works are great and marvelous – no one else can even come close to his works. His ways are righteous and true – everything God does is right and matches up 100% to the plumb line of truth. Line up truth and God's ways for an eternity, and there is no variation and no offset. You follow God's ways, and after an eternity, you will still be in line with the truth. You follow my ways, and after a minute, you are offline from the truth. Whose ways are you going to choose to follow? So, who will not fear the Lord and glorify His name? It is only His power that is great and marvelous, His ways that are right and true. He alone is holy. His righteous acts have been revealed in the death, burial, and resurrection of His son, so all the nations will come and worship before Him! What a song!

THE TEMPLE IN HEAVEN

15:5, After this, I looked, and I saw in heaven the temple—that is, the tabernacle of the covenant law—and it was opened. 6, Out of the temple came the seven angels with the seven plagues. They were dressed in clean, shining linen and wore golden sashes around their chests. 7, Then one of the four living creatures gave to the seven angels seven golden bowls filled with the wrath of God, who lives forever and ever. 8, And the temple was filled with smoke from the glory of God and from his power, and no one could enter the temple until the seven plagues of the seven angels were completed.

John sees in His vision that in heaven, the temple is very specifically related to the Tabernacle built by Moses in the desert. Moses was given extremely specific plans to build the Tabernacle, which was a copy of the temple in heaven.[CXXXI] This, in the Old Testament, was where God resided in solitude because He was Holy. The Holy of Holies was closed off by a heavy curtain and entered only once a year by a single high priest. Now, since Jesus was crucified, the door is open. As we've seen, this is where the Saints are![CXXXII]

Out of this temple came seven angels who carried the seven last plagues. Their raiment was that of priests, being clean white, shining linen with golden sashes around their chests. One of the living creatures that worship God constantly took a break from His worship to give the seven angels each a bowl that is filled with the wrath of God as if that were a catalyst to the plagues they carried with them.

God, who lives forever and ever, resides in the temple, and now, since His fury is being spent, the temple is filled with smoke from His magnificent glory and awesome power. This very same thing is spoken of several times in the Old Testament. When the tabernacle was completed,[CXXXIII] at the time of Korah's rebellion,[CXXXIV] and when the ark of the covenant was brought into the temple that Solomon built.[CXXXV] It is pictured once in Ezekiel 43 when God's glory returns to the temple after his glory had left the temple in Ezekiel 10. The smoke of God's glory would remain in the temple such that no one could enter until the judgment was complete. This is God's judgment. No one else is responsible. God is showing His full engagement in the judgment of those who have not come to Him for refuge.

THE SEVEN BOWLS OF GOD'S WRATH

THE FIRST TWO ANGELS

16:1, Then I heard a loud voice from the temple saying to the seven angels, "Go, pour out the seven bowls of God's wrath on the earth." 2, The first angel went and poured out his bowl on the land, and ugly, festering sores broke out on the people who had the mark of the beast and worshiped its image. 3, The second angel poured out his bowl on the sea, and it turned into blood like that of a dead person, and every living thing in the sea died.

The first two bowls are poured out over the land and the sea. The wrath poured out on the land affects all the people who have the mark of the beast and worship its image. Very much like the similar plagues in Egypt, this plague does not affect those who are God's people.[CXXXVI] The wrath poured out on the sea, turning it into blood like that of a dead person. In the seal judgment, one-fourth of everything living in the sea died; in the trumpet judgment, one-third died, but in the bowl judgment, everything died. God's judgment is no longer limited. Please reference the graph showing *The Three Representations of God's Judgement* at the end of this chapter.

THE THIRD ANGEL

16:4, The third angel poured out his bowl on the rivers and springs of water, and they became blood. 5, Then I heard the angel in charge of the waters say:

"You are just in these judgments, O Holy One,
you who are and who were;
6, for they have shed the blood of your holy people and your prophets,
and you have given them blood to drink as they deserve."

7, And I heard the altar respond:

"Yes, Lord God Almighty,
true and just are your judgments."

The third angel poured out his bowl on all the fresh waters of the earth, and they, too, became blood. In short, if you shed the blood of the innocent, you get blood to drink. It is just, and God is to be glorified because He does not neglect justice. How could a righteous God allow such atrocities to be brought upon His people without bringing justice upon those who caused his people to suffer? Here, we notice that the altar responds to this with praise to God, for true and just are his judgments. Now, it seems clear that it was not the altar that responded but those who were "under the altar" asking for God to bring justice upon their persecutors.[CXXXVII]

THE FOURTH AND FIFTH ANGELS

16:8, The fourth angel poured out his bowl on the sun, and the sun was allowed to scorch people with fire. 9, They were seared by the intense heat, and they cursed the name of God, who had control over these plagues, but they refused to repent and glorify him. 10, The fifth angel poured out his bowl on the throne of the beast, and its kingdom was plunged into darkness. People gnawed their tongues in agony 11, and cursed the God of heaven because of their pains and their sores, but they refused to repent of what they had done.

The fourth angel pours out his bowl on the sun, making it so hot that it sears people's skin, and yet when the fifth angel pours out his bowl on the throne of the beast and his kingdom, it is plunged into darkness. Everything is against the beast, both light and the lack thereof. The people who belong to his kingdom are in great agony, and they know the source of their pain, but they are unwilling, or maybe now unable, to repent of their sins and be spared all the agony. Once again, this is a vision and representative, not literal. All people, Christian or otherwise, have difficulty, pain, and suffering in this life on earth. For the rebellious person, it is a judgment, but for the Christian, it is for our strengthening. The rebellious ones are supposed to get the message that they need to repent and so be saved, but they will have none of it. Don't be like that. Be chastened by your suffering and turn ever more to God in obedience and love!

THE SIXTH ANGEL

16:12, The sixth angel poured out his bowl on the great river Euphrates, and its water was dried up to prepare the way for the kings from the East. 13, Then I saw three impure spirits that looked like frogs; they came out of the mouth of the dragon, out of the mouth of the beast, and out of the mouth of the false prophet. 14, They are demonic spirits that perform signs, and they go out to the kings of the whole world to gather them for the battle on the great day of God Almighty. 15, "Look, I come like a thief! Blessed is the one who stays awake and remains clothed so as not to go naked and be shamefully exposed." 16, Then they gathered the kings together at the place that in Hebrew is called Armageddon.

The sixth angel poured out his bowl on the Euphrates River so that it would dry up completely. This is God's action to open the way for the kings of the East to have an easy path to come to war. Satan isn't so bright; he thinks this is his chance to gather all the kings to fight against God. He sends the impure spirits - frogs, from the unholy trinity - the dragon, the beast, and the false prophet - to go and gather the kings for battle. The frogs are demonic spirits that perform signs to deceive and convince the kings of the whole world to gather for battle at a place called Armageddon.

Armageddon is a place of great biblical importance. It is a reference to the mount of Megiddo, where Deborah and Barak defeated Sisera's military, as told in Judges 4. See Deborah's song in Judges 5, especially verses 19-21. It is near there that Saul and Jonathon died in battle with the Philistines.[CXXXVIII] It is the place where King Josiah was killed by Pharaoh Necho in battle.[CXXXIX] The imagery here is that every king is coming here to fight a battle. I don't care how big the place is. It isn't big enough for every king to bring his army. There is another point to this.

Look who doesn't come to battle. It is those who are blessed (our third blessing of seven) because they stay awake and remain clothed. They will not go naked and be shamefully exposed by appearing in a battle against God. Hmmm, they won't be in the battle for God, either. He is capable of winning this battle all on his own. Don't you want to be associated with a God like that?

What exactly does it mean to keep our clothes about us so that we won't be found naked? I can't help thinking about a song by Jewel Kilcher called *Little Sister* that has the following lyrics, *...clothing is the closest approximation To God...*[CXL] I'm not smart enough to know all that Jewel had in mind when she wrote those lyrics, but I do know that when Adam and Eve sinned and broke their relationship with God, they suddenly needed clothes. Then, in Galatians 3:27, we find out that when we are baptized into Christ, we are clothed with Christ. Therefore, the first step to not being found naked is to choose to be baptized into Christ.

THE SEVENTH ANGEL

16:17, The seventh angel poured out his bowl into the air, and out of the temple came a loud voice from the throne, saying, "It is done!" 18, Then there came flashes of lightning, rumblings, peals of thunder, and a severe earthquake. No earthquake like it has ever occurred since mankind has been on earth, so tremendous was the quake. 19, The great city split into three parts, and the cities of the nations collapsed. God remembered Babylon the Great and gave her the cup filled with the wine of the fury of his wrath. 20, Every island fled away, and the mountains could not be found. 21, From the sky, huge hailstones, each weighing about a hundred pounds, fell on people. And they cursed God on account of the plague of hail because the plague was so terrible.

Now, the seventh angel pours out his bowl into the air. The first result of the pouring out of this bowl that we experience is the flashing of lightning, the sound of peals of thunder, and the greatest earthquake of all time. This is the answer to the prayers of the saints that we read about in Revelation 8:1-5. Look at it again and notice the similarities between the answer to their prayer there in verse 5 and here in verse 18. But now we see the real results of that prayer – the great city, perhaps Jerusalem, being split into three parts; the cities of the nations fall; Babylon, representing the current ruling nation, gets the full dose of God's wrath; the islands and mountains are destroyed; great hailstones fall on the people. The end has come for the nations who do not fear the Lord, and it is a representation of the coming judgment, which is when everyone who does not fear the Lord will face judgment.

When Jesus was hanging on the cross, he said seven phrases, the last of which was, "It is finished." Similarly, as the last of the seven plagues is poured out, God says, "It is done." Notice that the voice comes out of the temple from the throne where God resides, so this is God speaking. Jesus said the job was finished, and the necessary process was completed when he died on the cross. Here, God says that there has been a change of the state of being on the earth. Up until this time, there has always been an offer of repentance. Now that offer has been rescinded. Those who did not repent before this time wore out their welcome. They have now been judged, and there is no possibility of restoration.

Notice this. In this short chapter 16, which relates the pouring out of the bowls of God's wrath, we are given three verses relating to the response of the people on the earth. The first is in verse 9. They cursed the name of God, who had control over the plagues, and **they did not repent** to give Him glory. The second is in verse 11. They cursed the God of heaven because of their pain and their sores, and **they did not repent** of their deeds. The final time is in verse 21. They cursed God because of the plague of hail because the hailstone plague was extremely severe. Notice in verse 21 that there is no mention of repentance. That opportunity is no longer offered. It is done.

Have you heard the gospel? Jesus is God's son who came to earth as a baby – fully God and fully human. He taught us who God is both by his words and actions. He allowed himself to be crucified for our sins. He died and was buried for three days. He rose from the dead, and after 40 days of showing himself to many witnesses that he was alive, he ascended into heaven, where he intercedes for those who are his. Have you believed this message? Have you repented of your sins? Have you confessed Jesus as Lord? Have you been immersed in water for the forgiveness of your sins and to receive the gift of the Holy Spirit, at which time God will add you to Jesus' church? Have you walked in the light of God's word to the best of your ability, praying for forgiveness when you've come up short? If these things are true for you, then this judgment is not yours. Jesus will bring you safely home to be with him in Heaven. If these things are not true for you, do not delay making it so. Today is the day of salvation.

Table 10: Three Representations of God's Judgement

Angel Number	Seven Seals	Seven Trumpets	Seven Bowls
Reference	Revelation 6, 8	Revelation 8, 9, 11	Revelation 16
Purpose	Seals Reveal	Trumpets Announce	Bowls pour out or execute
Affect	Limited (The third horseman told not to damage the oil and wind, the fourth horseman given power over one-fourth of the earth)	One Third	Complete – Judgement affects everyone who has the mark of the beast
1st Angel	White horse – Conquest of earth.	Hail, fire, and blood on earth.	Painful boils on the people of the earth.

2nd Angel	Red horse – war-producing blood.	The sea became blood.	The sea became blood.
3rd Angel	Black horse – Famine probably resulting from the war.	Fresh water became bitter.	Fresh water became blood.
4th Angel	Pale horse – Death and Hades; death resulting from war, famine, plague, and wild animals.	The sun, moon, and stars turned dark.	Sun is given the power to scorch people with fire.
5th Angel	Martyrs crying out to God to judge their persecutors.	The Abyss opened, and locusts were given power to torture the unfaithful.	The Beast and his kingdom plunged into darkness.
6th Angel	The sun turns black, the Moon turns blood red, Stars fall from the sky, and every island and mountain is removed from its place.	Great army releases to kill mankind.	The River Euphrates dried up, making way for the armies of kings from the East.
7th Angel	Silence in heaven; Release of the seven trumpets.	Loud voices in heaven: "Now the kingdom of the world has become the kingdom of our Lord and of his Christ."	Everything is affected – a loud voice from the throne, "It is done!"

As you look back at the three representations of God's judgment, you will notice that for the Seals and the Trumpets, the first four angels were described quickly and with few words, but the following three were meticulously detailed. For the bowls, however, the first 5 are described quickly and with few words, and the final two are only a little more detailed. Also, between the 6th and 7th Seals and the 6th and 7th Trumpets, there was a significant delay. Now, in the Bowls, there is only a slight delay between the 3rd and 4th Bowls and the 6th and 7th Bowls. This is consistent with the prophecy in Revelation 10:6 that there would be no more delay.

CHAPTER 12

THE PROSTITUTE

Revelation 17:1 to 18:24.

John is greatly astonished by the next vision he sees. Part of this could be from what he has just seen. He is told that it is done. Judgment is complete and has taken place. But now he sees a great prostitute riding a great beast with all the appearances of great power and being fully alive and free to do what she wants to do, which includes persecuting God's people. Since Revelation 11:1, John has been in Jerusalem (in the Spirit), where he went to measure the temple. Now, at the time of John's visions and writing, the temple in Jerusalem had already been destroyed by Rome. This is a book that uses figurative language. Do not be confused by it, but be aware of it. Also, be aware that all the things John saw from then until now were from that vantage point. He saw angels coming "down from heaven." Now, one of the seven-bowl angels takes him (in the Spirit) to a desert area still on earth. What we see from now on until Revelation 21:9 is from this desert vantage point.

As we continue through our study of these two chapters of Revelation, you will find the following table useful as it compares the beasts.

Table 11: Comparing the Beasts

Dragon	Sea Beast	Prostitute's Beast	Interpretations
Revelation 12:3,4	Revelation 13:1-9	Revelation 17:3,8	Revelation 17:9-12
Red color		Scarlet color	
	Out of the Sea	Out of the Abyss	
Seven heads	Seven heads	Seven heads	Seven hills, Seven kings
Seven crowns on his heads	Blasphemous name on each head	Covered with blasphemous names	
Defeated and awaiting ultimate defeat	One head had a fatal wound that was healed	Once was, now is not, yet will come (but goes to his destruction)	The eighth king who belongs to the seven is going to his destruction
Ten horns	Ten horns; Ten crowns on his horns	Ten horns	Ten kings who have not yet received a kingdom
Enormous, tail swept a third of the stars out of the sky, Ancient serpent, Devil, Satan, leads the whole world astray	Resembled a leopard, feet like a bear, the mouth of a lion, power, and authority derived from the dragon	Beast and Ten Horns will hate the prostitute and destroy her	

REVELATION 17 BREAKDOWN

The sea beast on which the woman sits has seven heads, which are said to be seven hills on which the woman sits and seven kings. Of the seven kings, 5 have fallen, the sixth currently is, and the seventh is yet to come. The beast that has these seven heads once was, but currently, it is not. The beast will reappear for some time as an eighth king before going to its destruction.

I. The Prostitute
1. Sits on:
    a. Many waters: Peoples, multitudes, nations, and languages.
    b. The beast: the current governing authority.
    c. Seven hills or mountains.
2. Dressed:
    a. In purple and scarlet
    b. Has jewelry made of glittering gold, precious stones, and pearls.
3. Drinking:
    a. From a golden cup
    b. Abominable things
    c. The filth of her adulteries
    d. Drunk with the blood of the saints and those who bore testimony of Jesus.
4. Title "Mystery":
    a. Babylon the Great
    b. The mother of prostitutes
    c. The mother of the abominations of the earth.
5. Identity: The great city that rules over the kings of the earth
6. Kings of the earth committed adultery with her.

II.   Seven Heads

    1.   Seven hills on which the woman sits.

    2.   Seven kings

        a.   Five kings have fallen.

        b.   The sixth king currently is.

        c.   The seventh one is yet to come.

        d.   The eighth king is the beast resurrected.

III.   Ten kings

    1.   They will receive authority for one hour with the beast.

    2.   Their purpose is to give power and authority to the beast.

    3.   They make war against the Lamb.

JOHN'S VISION

17:1, One of the seven angels who had the seven bowls came and said to me, "Come, I will show you the punishment of the great prostitute, who sits by many waters. 2, With her, the kings of the earth committed adultery, and the inhabitants of the earth were intoxicated with the wine of her adulteries."

3, Then the angel carried me away in the Spirit into a wilderness. There, I saw a woman sitting on a scarlet beast that was covered with blasphemous names and had seven heads and ten horns. 4, The woman was dressed in purple and scarlet and was glittering with gold, precious stones, and pearls. She held a golden cup in her hand, filled with abominable things and the filth of her adulteries. 5, The name written on her forehead was a mystery:

Babylon the Great, the mother of prostitutes and of the abominations of the earth. 6, I saw that the woman was drunk with the blood of God's holy people, the blood of those who bore testimony to Jesus.

When I saw her, I was greatly astonished.

Yes, an angel who had one of the seven bowls tells John that he will see the punishment of the great prostitute, but he hasn't seen that yet, and his astonishment arose. We are told that the kings of the earth committed adultery with her. This would seem to indicate that this prostitute is a state that is the center of financial trade throughout the world. God used similar terms when speaking of Assyria when they were a big deal in trade.[CXLI] On the other hand, Israel was spoken of as a spiritual prostitute in their constantly seeking after idols and the pagan gods of other nations.[CXLII]

This prostitute is sitting on a beast. The beast is scarlet in color from the blood it has shed, and it has blasphemous names written all over it because its character is to blaspheme God. It has seven heads and ten horns, just like the dragon and the beast we saw coming up out of the sea. The prostitute is in league with Satan, corrupt government, and corrupt religion. Well, all that and a corrupt financial system. She is rich – look at what she wears. She has a beautiful, expensive robe. She's glittering from head to toe in gold, precious stones, and pearls. All this wealth has come because she is in league with Satan and these corrupt entities. But they have come at the expense of God's people – she is drunk on their blood. I'd be astonished, too! One thing that would astonish me is that God would allow such things to happen to his people. Why does God allow such wickedness to flourish? We have but to remain faithful, whatever may come.

THE ANGEL'S EXPLANATION

17:7, Then the angel said to me: "Why are you astonished? I will explain to you the mystery of the woman and of the beast she rides, which has seven heads and ten horns. 8, The beast, which you saw, once was, now is not, and yet will come up out of the Abyss and go to its destruction. The inhabitants of the earth whose names have not been written in the Book of Life from the creation of the world will be astonished when they see the beast because it once was, now is not, and yet will come.

The angel says, "Don't be astonished." It is not fitting for a child of God to be astonished at one who was, now is not, and yet will come again. We worship a God who did just that in two ways. Jesus walked the earth, died, and "was not" for three days and came back from the dead. Jesus was on earth; he ascended into heaven, and "now is not" but will come again. This beast is a counterfeit Christ and Messiah. The world that does not know these things will be astonished when they see God's things counterfeited, but those whose names are written in the Book of Life should not be astonished because they have been adequately forewarned. If the beast represents a persecuting government, then the people that John is writing to are experiencing a temporary reprieve and are being warned that it will soon rise again. The beast once persecuted them, but now it is not, and it will soon be again.

17:9, "This calls for a mind with wisdom. The seven heads are seven hills on which the woman sits. 10, They are also seven kings. Five have fallen; one is, the other has not yet come, but when he does come, he must remain for only a little while. 11 The beast who once was, and now is not, is an eighth king. He belongs to the seven and is going to his destruction.

Theories abound about who these eight kings are. Do they represent the kings of Rome? Augustus, Tiberius, Caligula, Claudius, Nero, Vespasian, Titus, and Domitian. Do they represent empires that afflicted God's people? Egypt, Assyria, Babylonia, Medo-Persia, Greece, Rome, and two others. Does it matter? One thing is needed: The wisdom to remain faithful to the God of the universe, who has all things under his control. The wisdom to put one's faith and trust in Him, who created all things and has an amazing plan of salvation. When things don't make any earthly sense, heavenly trust is needed.

17:12, "The ten horns you saw are ten kings who have not yet received a kingdom, but who for one hour will receive authority as kings along with the beast. 13, They have one purpose and will give their power and authority to the beast. 14,

They will wage war against the Lamb, but the Lamb will triumph over them because He is Lord of lords and King of kings—and with Him will be called, His chosen and faithful followers."

Consider that in the grand scheme of time, every king that has ever existed has had authority for only one hour. Any king or governor who gives their power and authority to the beast is doomed to be brought to judgment. Haven't we seen this repeatedly in history? Governments such as this are constantly waging war against the Lamb and His faithful followers. But the Lamb always triumphs over them because He is Lord of lords and King of kings. His chosen and faithful followers get to enjoy the victory.

Don't be misled by these things looking for some end-times calendar to tell you when Jesus will return. We will not know that until the day and hour that it happens. Then everyone will know. Read 1 and 2 Thessalonians and 2 Peter. Jesus' return will come like a thief in the night. Thieves do not announce their coming. They don't call ahead. It just calls for us to be faithful and ready. It calls for us to be faithful and wise servants, feeding our fellowmen spiritually and taking care of each other physically until Jesus comes in all his glory. Let's commit together to be that kind of people.

17:15, Then the angel said to me, "The waters you saw, where the prostitute sits, are peoples, multitudes, nations, and languages. 16, The beast and the ten horns you saw will hate the prostitute. They will bring her to ruin and leave her naked; they will eat her flesh and burn her with fire. 17, For God has put it into their hearts to accomplish his purpose by agreeing to hand over to the beast their royal authority until God's words are fulfilled. 18, The woman you saw is the great city that rules over the kings of the earth."

The prostitute is identified as the great city that rules over the kings of the earth. At the time of John's vision, this could only have been Rome. Before we go on, my question for your consideration is, does this mean that Revelation is limited to refer only to Rome? Could it not be referring to any great earthly city, state, or country that rules over the kings of the earth in a given age? I think, yes. In any case, the prostitute is supported by the waters she sits on – the people she rules over, by the beast – the current governing authority, and by the ten horns – kings with limited authority. All three of these entities hate her because she rules over them ruthlessly. One mistake, and into her cup you go! The great city cannot sustain itself without those she rules over, so when they revolt, she is stripped of her wealth and destroyed.

THE FALL OF BABYLON – The Agony of Defeat

18:1, After this I saw another angel coming down from heaven. He had great authority, and the earth was illuminated by his splendor. 2, With a mighty voice he shouted:

> *"'Fallen! Fallen is Babylon the Great!'*
> *She has become a dwelling for demons*
> *and a haunt for every impure spirit,*
> *a haunt for every unclean bird,*
> *a haunt for every unclean and detestable animal.*
> *3, For all the nations have drunk*
> *the maddening wine of her adulteries.*
> *The kings of the earth committed adultery with her,*
> *and the merchants of the earth grew rich from her excessive luxuries."*

Many commentators say that the use of the term Babylon as code for Rome was so that the governing authorities of Rome would not know what was being spoken of and thus would not destroy those who carried the message. That may be true to some extent, but I prefer that Babylon is code for any government that sets itself up against God. Any government that does so has started the clock to its demise. Here, the angel rejoices over the destruction of the prostitute – over the fall of Babylon. The result of her demise is that she is desolate and

empty. Only witches and demons and their ilk go there now —
she is haunted. She hadn't been alone before. The nations
shared in drinking the wine of her adulteries. The kings of the
earth envied her riches, so they committed adultery with her
because they wanted to share in her wealth.

What were Babylon's adulteries? She put worldly wealth
and the pleasures of sin as her top priorities. Her wealth was
amassed at the expense of her concern for the people who
supplied her wealth. She traded by manipulation and greed, not
out of a heart for service and love. She was ruthless, proud,
ungodly, idolatrous. This is maddening wine! Everyone who
indulges in this lifestyle is ruled by it to their own emotional,
social, and ultimately spiritual detriment.

This is a powerful and important message. The angel that
delivered it came down out of heaven. He had great authority.
The earth was illuminated by His glory! This angel has as close
an association with God as you can get. How else could he have
such great authority and the ability to illuminate the earth with
His glory? His message is being delivered directly from God with
no delay. Remember how Moses' face would shine after being
in God's presence, and it would diminish over time?[CXLIII] There
was no time for this angel to lose the shining glory of God — the
message was urgent and quickly delivered.

THE CALL TO GOD'S PEOPLE

18:4, Then I heard another voice from heaven say:

> *"'Come out of her, my people,'*
> *so that you will not share in her sins,*
> *so that you will not receive any of her plagues;*
> *5, for her sins are piled up to heaven,*
> *and God has remembered her crimes.*
> *6, Give back to her as she has given;*
> *pay her back double for what she has done.*
> *Pour her a double portion from her own cup.*
> *7, Give her as much torment and grief*

God's people are called to come out of Babylon. What is the Babylon of your generation? For those in John's day, it was Rome. For those in Daniel's day, it was literally Babylon. But were they called to literally leave those cities? No, because wherever there are people, there will be sin. God is not calling us to live as monks. They were called to mentally, emotionally, and spiritually leave those cities. Do not share in their sins. Do not share in their pleasures. Do not love what they love. Do not defend their evil lifestyles. Live as strangers and pilgrims on earth, looking for a new home in heaven.

This is figurative language relating to what God told those living in Jerusalem before its demise by Rome. Matthew, speaking of Rome's destruction of Jerusalem, indicates that when a person saw Rome's military headed toward Jerusalem, they should leave immediately so as not to be caught up in the effects of God's judgment on Jerusalem via Rome's military.[CXLIV] That is what we're seeing here in Revelation 18:4 in a figurative sense since when judgment comes now, it'll be universal destruction – that is, the destruction of the whole universe.[CXLV]

Why should we separate ourselves from whatever today's Babylon is? That city's sins are piled up in one awful pile of stench all the way to heaven. God remembers their sins because how could he forget them? The stench is affecting even his nostrils. Thus, the angel now presents the judgment against Babylon. Give back to her as she has given. Pay her back double for what she has done. Pour out for her a double portion of her own evil. Those who lead people astray, abuse people, use people as means to their own pleasure and wealth, and those who have filled up the full measure of their disobedience to God will experience the full measure of God's wrath upon them. There is no free lunch for consuming the people that God has made in His own image and put on earth to do good to each other and to learn the ways of God, but are deceived by the pleasures and depravity of sin that the prostitute puts forth as desirable and good. She gave herself glory and luxury – they were not received by service but by deceit, so she will receive back just as much in torment and grief.

The prostitute is deceived. She thinks that she will get to live in her self-proclaimed glory and luxury forever. She is so drunk with her pleasures that she doesn't see the end coming. It comes suddenly. Before she knows it, all her luxury and pleasure will be removed from her. In one moment, death, mourning, and famine will strike her on the face, and she, along with all the heavenly bodies, earthly bodies, kingdoms of men, and anything physical, will be burned up in intense heat in an all-consuming fire. That will be it for her.

Need I say it again? I remember as a child watching Pete Rose A.K.A. Charlie Hustle, run to first base to beat out a throw. He was amazing. He gave it everything he got when it came to baseball. Doesn't this story of the prostitute make you want to run like Pete Rose away from all the so-called pleasures, glory, and luxury offered by the prostitute and toward all the true joy that comes from a life submitted to Christ? A life that will not burn up in the intense heat of His return. I sure hope you make every effort not to be caught up in the destruction of the prostitute when it happens.

THE COLLATERAL DAMAGE OF BABYLON'S FALL

18:9, "When the kings of the earth who committed adultery with her and shared her luxury see the smoke of her burning, they will weep and mourn over her. 10, Terrified at her torment, they will stand far off and cry:

> *"'Woe! Woe to you, great city,*
> *You mighty city of Babylon!*
> *In one hour, your doom has come!'*

11, "The merchants of the earth will weep and mourn over her because no one buys their cargoes anymore— 12, cargoes of gold, silver, precious stones, and pearls; fine linen, purple, silk and scarlet cloth; every sort of citron wood, and articles of every kind made of ivory, costly wood, bronze, iron and marble; 13, cargoes of cinnamon and spice, of incense, myrrh and frankincense, of wine and olive oil, of fine flour and wheat; cattle and sheep; horses and carriages; and human beings sold as slaves.

14, "They will say, 'The fruit you longed for is gone from you. All your luxury and splendor have vanished, never to be recovered.' 15, The merchants who sold these things and gained their wealth from her will stand far off, terrified at her torment. They will weep and mourn 16, and cry out:

> *"'Woe! Woe to you, great city,*
> *dressed in fine linen, purple and scarlet,*
> *and glittering with gold, precious stones and pearls!*
> *17, In one hour, such great wealth has been brought to ruin!'*

"Every sea captain, and all who travel by ship, the sailors, and all who earn their living from the sea, will stand far off. 18, When they see the smoke of her burning, they will exclaim, 'Was there ever a city like this great city?' 19, They will throw dust on their heads and, with weeping and mourning, cry out:

> *"'Woe! Woe to you, great city,*
> *where all who had ships on the sea*
> *became rich through her wealth!*
> *In one hour, she has been brought to ruin!'*

It's not a good day for the prostitute, Babylon. In one hour (figurative language), she has been brought to ruin. She's come to her demise, and now look at what her friends say and do. Her first group of friends are the kings of Earth. They committed adultery with her and enjoyed her luxury, but now they stand far off. So much for friendship! They are nowhere near to helping the poor prostitute in all her suffering. At least they feel sorry for her, right? They cry over her and mourn for her, but their crying and mourning are selfish. They are crying and mourning over the fact that they no longer have the prostitute to commit adultery with. They have lost the source of the luxury they were living in.

Her second group of friends are the merchants of the earth. They, too, stand far off from the prostitute who bought all their cargo. She has made them rich by buying all their wonderful products, which she used for her trade in luxury, adultery, and prostitution. Check out Ezekiel 27. Words similar to these were spoken about Tyre. (The interesting thing is that it was Babylon that was supposed to inflict these sufferings on Tyre! Nebuchadnezzar of Babylon laid siege against Tyre for 13 years, from 586 BC to 573 BC. It wasn't until 332 BC that Alexander the Great succeeded in removing Tyre from the earth. This was only temporary, however, as Rome rebuilt Tyre some years later.) But these merchants are selfish, just like the kings of the earth. They didn't care about the prostitute; they were in love with the wealth they received from her. Now their source of wealth is gone, and they are in mourning – not for her, but for themselves.

Her third group of friends are all those who earn their living by the sea and sell her their wares. I bet you can't guess where they are! Oh, you're right! They, too, stand far off. They aren't willing to come close to helping either. What does this group ask? "Was there ever a city like this great city?" Are we talking about Rome here? Of course, she is unique, but not entirely so. She is being called "Babylon" because of her similarity to that city. We just saw that the lament of the merchants at the loss of Rome (Babylon) matched the lament of Tyre. Over the course of history, many cities have been in control of most of the people of Earth. What city, or cities, in our day would be considered Babylon?

In Star Trek Next Generation, there is a scene where the android, Data, drinks alcohol with his emotion chip turned on. He has an amusingly negative response to the taste and effect that it has on him. His words are, "I hate this. It's revolting!" Guinan asks if he wants more, and he responds, "Please." That's what we see in these people standing back and seeing the destruction of the prostitute. They are revolted by what has happened to the prostitute, but they want more!

THE AUTOPSY OF BABYLON

18:20, "Rejoice over her, you heavens!
Rejoice, you people of God!
Rejoice, apostles and prophets!
For God has judged her
with the judgment she imposed on you."

21, Then a mighty angel picked up a boulder the size of a large millstone and threw it into the sea, and said:

"With such violence
The great city of Babylon will be thrown down,
never to be found again.
22, The music of harpists and musicians, pipers, and
trumpeters,
will never be heard in you again.
No worker of any trade
will ever be found in you again.
The sound of a millstone
will never be heard in you again.
23, The light of a lamp
will never shine in you again.
The voice of bridegroom and bride

When the prostitute, Babylon, falls, the heavens rejoice. The people of God rejoice. The apostles and prophets rejoice. They are commanded to rejoice because the prostitute is judged for the way she treats them. As she has imposed judgment on God's people, she is now judged. That is cause for celebration. When God gives you a victory, do not be too demure to rejoice in it. It may not have anything to do with anything you did, but God did it for you. Celebrate!

Now for an object lesson. A mighty angel picks up a boulder the size of a large millstone (For those of us in the 21st century, that's big!) and tosses it into the sea. The angel says that with violence such as this, the great city of Babylon is thrown down. It will never be found again. This is not as hard to understand as people think. Have we found where Babylon used to be? Yes. Will it ever be a ruling city again? No. If Babylon refers to Rome, have we lost Rome? Of course not. But Rome will never rule the world again. If Babylon refers to Israel, have we lost Israel? Of course not, but Israel will never be the ruling city it could have been. We have seen this in many of the ruling cities and nations that God has judged. Egypt, Syria, Assyria, Tyre. Nations and cities that abused God's people rather than serve the Lord and that God has judged and said they will disappear, never to be found again. Many still exist but have never returned to prominence and never will.

Notice the symmetry of chapter 18. It starts with an angel predicting Babylon's fall and ends with an angel's actions and words describing Babylon's fall. After the prediction of Babylon's fall, a voice from heaven is heard warning God's people, and before the description of Babylon's fall, the saints are admonished to rejoice. In between these four events are the three pictures of the response to Babylon's fall by those who joined in her prostitution. Seven voices, each from a different source, experience the fall of the prostitute, Babylon.

Since the prostitute is sure to fall, in whatever age she exists, should we not take seriously the admonition to separate ourselves from her? We know her time is short, and we don't want to be found staring at her demise from a far-off location, wishing we could still be engaging in her prostitution. We want to be of the group that knew it was coming, separated ourselves from her spiritually, and rejoice in the salvation we experience when her certain demise comes about. The one purpose of the book of Revelation is heart change. Period. Will you change your heart to be the Lord's, not Babylon's? Will you flee Babylon and all her luxuriant prostitution and run toward Jesus and His righteousness? That is what this book is about. Giving us the motivation to flee whatever belongs to Babylon and run toward whatever belongs to the Lord.

CHAPTER 13

THE RIDER

Revelation 19:1 to 20:10.

We saw in the previous chapter that the saints were commanded to rejoice. Those who were in bed with the prostitute Babylon were not rejoicing. But those who refused to join in on her adulteries show their separation from her by rejoicing at her fall. This is not childish laughing in the face of the person bullying you when they trip. This is the rejoicing of those who are saved from the oppressor in the greatest battle ever and for all time. God has brought victory to His people through the lamb, so rejoicing and worship are in order.

THE HALLELUJAH CHORUS

19:1, After this, I heard what sounded like the roar of a great multitude in heaven shouting: "Hallelujah! Salvation and glory and power belong to our God, 2, for true and just are his judgments. He has condemned the great prostitute who corrupted the earth by her adulteries. He has avenged on her the blood of his servants." 3, And again they shouted: "Hallelujah! The smoke from her goes up forever and ever." 4, The twenty-four elders and the four living creatures fell down and worshiped God, who was seated on the throne. And they cried: "Amen, Hallelujah!" 5, Then a voice came from the throne, saying: "Praise our God, all you his servants, you who fear him, both great and small!" 6, Then I heard what sounded like a great multitude, like the roar of rushing waters and like loud peals of thunder, shouting: "Hallelujah! For our Lord God Almighty reigns. 7, Let us rejoice and be glad and give him glory! For the wedding of the Lamb has come, and his bride has made herself ready. 8, Fine linen, bright and clean, was given her to wear." (Fine linen stands for the righteous acts of God's holy people.)

9, Then the angel said to me, "Write this: Blessed are those who are invited to the wedding supper of the Lamb!" And he added, "These are the true words of God." 10 At this, I fell at his feet to worship him. But he said to me, "Don't do that! I am a fellow servant with you and with your brothers and sisters who hold to the testimony of Jesus. Worship God! For it is the Spirit of prophecy who bears testimony to Jesus."

In the previous chapter, we saw the condemnation and destruction of the prostitute. We saw the responses of those who committed adultery with her and observed that the response came from three sources: kings, land merchants, and sea merchants. We saw the figurative description of the current Babylon, Rome, after the fall. Those who remained holy to the Lord are commanded to rejoice, and now we see them obeying that command. In an interesting switch in numerology, there were three groups grieving the loss of the prostitute, and we see four hallelujahs of rejoicing because of the victory over her. Since she is of the earth, you would expect four groups to be mourning her loss, and since the victor over her is divine, you would expect hallelujah to be said three times.

In this Hallelujah Chorus, we see four hallelujahs. The first hallelujah comes from a great multitude in heaven. The second hallelujah comes again from the great multitude in heaven. The third hallelujah comes from the twenty-four elders and the four living creatures who constantly worship God on His throne. The fourth hallelujah again comes from a great multitude.

In the first hallelujah, we see these attributes of God: 1. Salvation belongs to him, 2. Glory belongs to him, 3. Power belongs to him, 4. His judgments are true, 5. His judgments are righteous, 6. He has judged the great prostitute, and 7. He has avenged the blood of the saints. We see these attributes of the prostitute: 1. She was corrupting the earth, 2. She engaged in sexual immorality; 3. She persecuted the saints to the death. Why, oh why, would one live for the pleasures offered by the prostitute when they are temporary, corrupt, and destructive? God's ways are the ways of eternal joy.

The second hallelujah says that the prostitute's destruction lasts forever. She, the current Babylon, will never be able to entice people to her adulteries again. There have been other Babylons since then. Each one offers temporary wealth and pleasures, but they are all temporary, deceptive, and destructive. Eventually, each one ends in everlasting destruction.

The third hallelujah, from the 24 elders and the four living creatures, is a simple "Amen," so be it. The prostitute got what she deserved for the corruption she caused. But there is a small interlude between the third and fourth hallelujah. A voice comes from the throne saying, "Give praise to our God." This voice probably came from one of the angels in the multitude of angels around the throne since they are calling for all the bondservants of God to bring praise to God. In any case, this is what the great multitude does again. They are so loud that it sounds like many waters and loud peals of thunder. They proclaim, exclaim, and loudly announce, "Hallelujah! For the Lord our God, the Almighty reigns." Don't you want to be in THAT chorus? Where else would you want to be? There is nowhere else anyone could want to be. Why would I allow anything to draw me away from my devotion to my Lord such that I would not be invited to join this chorus?

After the multitude's final Hallelujah, they continue with a statement about why we should worship God and the attitude we should have while doing so. We are to rejoice and be glad while we give glory to God because the marriage of the Lamb has come. We are now looking symbolically at the end of the world when the church, as the bride of Christ, is joined with Christ. Notice how the bride, who is the church, was prepared for the marriage. She prepared herself. The idea that salvation is done 100% by God without the saved person's faith, cooperation, and obedience is one of the most pernicious doctrines made by man. Hear the scripture. Predestination is a man-made doctrine. Everyone who has ever been saved since the creation of the world has chosen, of their own volition, to submit to God.

How did she prepare herself? Through righteous acts. Where did she get these righteous acts? From God. Now, neither God nor the Lamb did those acts for her. The Lamb told her what she needed to do to be righteous. He helped her do those acts of righteousness, but she still had to do them. The bride made herself ready. In this one little section, we see that grace-only salvation is refuted along with faith-only salvation. We are saved by grace through faith, Ephesians 2:8. Both God's grace to offer salvation and our response of faith to accept his gracious gift are required for salvation. The third idea, being grace through faith only, meaning my only part is to believe, is also refuted here. The bride had to make herself ready by her righteous acts. There is no salvation without obedience. Paul told us this in 2 Thessalonians 1:8, where he states that when Jesus returns, the criteria for being found faithful is to know God and to obey the gospel. If there is anything you do in this life, Know God and find out what it means to obey the gospel and do it.

In verse 9, we are seeing our fourth blessing of the seven of Revelation. Those who are invited to the wedding supper of the Lamb are blessed. Who are those who are invited? That must include the great multitude of worshipers that we see in the preceding 8 verses, those who are servants of God, as we see in verse 10. Those who hold to the testimony of Jesus. These people, angels, and creatures are blessed. This blessing isn't something the angel just observed to happen. These are the true words of God. This is His promise. This worship experience is so overwhelming to John that he falls down in worship of the mighty angel who is showing him these things. But no matter how glorious the servant is, the only one worthy of worship is God. The angel, though an amazing being in our eyes, sees himself as not beyond those who hold to the testimony of Jesus. The heart and aim of prophecy *is* Jesus, and that is what the angel was proclaiming. We who hold to the testimony of Jesus, though not having the special ability of prophecy, have an equal message. We are all servants of the most high God to share the message of Jesus.

Don't you want to be a member of the groups holding to the testimony of Jesus and, therefore, rejoicing and praising God? Wouldn't that be better than mourning the loss of an earthly benefactor that really didn't benefit you at all? They were all lies to make you a servant to her adulteries. Don't you want to be invited to the wedding supper of the Lamb? Wouldn't you want to be given a fresh new garment of fine linen, bright and clean? See how Revelation is about heart change? We see the terrible result of turning away from God and relying on earthly things versus the wonderful result of seeking the lamb. All the talk of what this or that symbolizes is fine, but it misses the real point. Put your hope in God and Christ and reap eternal joy, not in earthly things that result in eternal disaster.

THE RIDER ON THE WHITE HORSE

19:11, I saw heaven standing open, and there before me was a white horse, whose rider is called Faithful and True. With justice, he judges and wages war. 12, His eyes are like blazing fire, and on his head are many crowns. He has a name written on him that no one knows but he himself. 13, He is dressed in a robe dipped in blood, and his name is the Word of God. 14, The armies of heaven were following him, riding on white horses, and dressed in fine linen, white and clean. 15, Coming out of his mouth is a sharp sword with which to strike down the nations. "He will rule them with an iron scepter." He treads the winepress of the fury of the wrath of God Almighty. 16, On his robe and on his thigh, he has this name written: "king of kings and lord of lords."

17, And I saw an angel standing in the sun, who cried in a loud voice to all the birds flying in midair, "Come, gather together for the great supper of God, 18, so that you may eat the flesh of kings, generals, and the mighty, of horses and their riders, and the flesh of all people, free and slave, great and small."

19, Then I saw the beast and the kings of the earth and their armies gathered together to wage war against the rider on the horse and his army. 20, But the beast was captured, and with it, the false prophet who had performed the signs on its behalf. With these signs, he deluded those who had received the mark of the beast and worshiped its image. The two of them were thrown alive into the fiery lake of burning sulfur. 21, The rest were killed with the sword coming out of the mouth of the rider on the horse, and all the birds gorged themselves on their flesh.

Let's first look at the descriptions of the rider. His eyes are like a blazing fire, and he has a sharp, double-edged sword coming out of his mouth. We saw this description of the one like a son of man in Revelation chapter 1. There he was standing among the lampstands representing the churches, and here he is riding a white horse going out conquering and to conquer as in Revelation 6:2. Here we are told that he has many crowns on his head, not just 7 or 10 as the dragon and the sea beast had, respectively. In every way, Jesus is superior to the dragon and anyone in his posse. But we also see that he is dressed in a robe dipped in blood. His robe is dipped in the blood of his sacrifice on the cross and reminds us of the redemptive work of Jesus on the cross. The prostitute was drunk with the blood of God's holy people, but Jesus' robe was dipped in his own blood, which made them holy!

Now, let's focus on how he is identified. He is called Faithful and true. His name is the word of God. He has the name written: KING OF KINGS AND LORD OF LORDS. Compare this name with the name of the prostitute in Revelation 17:5, "Babylon the great, the mother of prostitutes and of the abominations of the earth." Which name is more attractive to you? Which one do you want to be associated with? Here's the trick of life – if you don't actively choose to be associated with the rider on the white horse, you have chosen to be associated with the prostitute. Make your choice wisely.

We are told that He has a name that no one knows but himself. This is similar in fashion to the song that only the saints could learn[CXLVI] because it is a song that only saints would sing. But how is it that we are told the rider's name in three ways, yet no one knows his name but him? His name is unique to him. No one else can wear that name. As unique as my name is, there are many people who have the same name, and I'm sure they wear it quite well, but no one can wear the name "Faithful and True," "The Word of God," "King of Kings and Lord of Lords" but Jesus, the Christ, the Son of the Living God. He is our one and only savior. Our only path to heaven.

Now, let's look at what the rider does. He judges and makes war with justice, and he rules the nations with an iron scepter. He doesn't play favorites. There is no way to buy his favor. He strikes down the nations with the sword of his mouth. The sword of his mouth is the word of God, and it is his implement of war. It is the word of God that judges us on the last day.[CXLVII] Then he treads the winepress of the fury of the wrath of God Almighty. This is another representation of the judgment we saw in Revelation 14:10 of those who worship the beast and his image – they will drink of the wine (that the rider here is pressing) of the wrath of God, which is mixed in full strength in the cup of His anger. See also Revelation 16:19, in which Babylon is given the cup of the wine of His fierce wrath.

Who is with him? The armies of heaven follow him. They are dressed in fine linen, white and clean. This is also the garb given to the bride of the Lamb! In verse 8, we learn that this fine linen stands for the righteous acts of the saints. So, the armies of heaven that follow him must be the Lamb's bride, the saints, those who are saved by His blood. This is not limited to 144,000 people. It is a great multitude.

Verses 17 and 18 are interesting. We understand from verse 9 that the saints are invited to the wedding supper of the Lamb, and collectively, as the church, they are his bride. Here, we see another invitation to a feast. This invitation is for the birds who will feast on those who are not invited to the wedding supper. Everyone is invited to a feast. The saints are invited to the wedding supper of the Lamb, and everyone else gets to be the supper of the birds by default. This sounds very morbid, but let that vision motivate you to do whatever is necessary to be invited to the Lamb's wedding supper and not to be the bird's supper.

Now that the suppers are prepared, the beast and all who have been deceived by him gather to make war on the Rider of the White Horse and all His armies. So, the battle is joined in verses 20 and 21, but what do the armies of the Rider do? Nothing. The beast and the false prophet are seized and thrown alive into the lake of fire that was prepared for them. All the armies that followed them were killed by the sword of the word of God that comes from the mouth of the rider, while His armies witnessed the great victory. Look, the defeat of God's enemy is complete and irrevocable. Make sure you are in His army.

THE THOUSAND YEARS

20:1, And I saw an angel coming down out of heaven, having the key to the Abyss and holding in his hand a great chain. 2, He seized the dragon, that ancient serpent, who is the devil, or Satan, and bound him for a thousand years. 3, He threw him into the Abyss and locked and sealed it over him to keep him from deceiving the nations anymore until the thousand years were ended. After that, he must be set free for a short time.

4, I saw thrones on which were seated those who had been given authority to judge. And I saw the souls of those who had been beheaded because of their testimony about Jesus and because of the word of God. They had not worshiped the beast or its image and had not received its mark on their foreheads or their hands. They came to life and reigned with Christ a thousand years. 5, (The rest of the dead did not come to life until the thousand years were ended.) This is the first resurrection. 6, Blessed and holy are those who share in the first resurrection. The second death has no power over them, but they will be priests of God and of Christ and will reign with him for a thousand years.

We have just read about the victory of Christ and his heavenly army, how the beast and the false prophet were thrown alive into the lake of fire while their armies were killed for the birds to feast upon. Now John sees an angel coming down from heaven who puts the dragon into the Abyss. Back in Revelation 9:1, we saw that a star that had fallen from heaven to earth was given the key to the abyss, and he opened it. Scorpions/locusts came from the abyss upon the earth and the people of the earth. These creatures from the abyss were not permitted to harm the people of God, yet they were under the king of the abyss, who goes by the name "destruction." This is the same abyss from which the beast came that killed the two prophets in Revelation 11:7. Also, the beast that was, and is not, and will be again, will come out of this abyss to go to his destruction. [CXLVIII] Satan will be locked in this abyss for 1000 years so that he cannot deceive anyone during that time. Doesn't it seem that the abyss is a place where all the evil beings are kept by God so that, for a time, they do not harm people? Don't we see that God is always in control, even of when and how much evil can be done? No matter what age we live in, evil is allowed to work to some extent and for some period of time. But God will always limit its effect and save those whose hearts are strong toward him.

Remember that we are in a vision. We have seen a dragon that represents Satan, we have seen a water beast that represents the nations, we have seen the land beast that represents false religion, and we've seen a prostitute that represents Babylon. We've seen the 144,000 righteous people who were symbolic of a much larger group, so it must be that the 1000 years spoken of here are also symbolic. The 1,000 years cannot be literal when everything around it is symbolic in the vision of John. Satan's activities are restricted while those who were beheaded for their testimony reign with Christ for 1000 years. The 1000 years represents the triumph of Christ and the irrevocable defeat of Satan and evil. Even though Satan's defeat is irrevocable, he is set free for a short time. Be aware! Be awake!

Let's consider the timeline given thus far in this chapter. When the prostitute, Babylon, Rome, if you like, is destroyed, there are several things that happen.

1. The beasts are thrown into the lake of fire.

2. The armies of Satan are killed.

3. Satan is locked in the abyss.

4. The beheaded souls are resurrected.

For the armies of Satan, this is the first death. For the beheaded souls, this is the first resurrection. Satan is bound for 1000 years while Christ and the resurrected souls reign for that same 1000 years. Those who reign with Christ, having experienced the first resurrection, will not taste the second death. Now let's see what happens after the 1000 years are over and Satan is allowed to go free for a time.

Before we do, notice that this section ends with our fifth of seven blessings. Blessed and holy are those who experience the first resurrection. They are blessed because they will not experience the second death. When the saints are resurrected, they live forever. This is important to our understanding of end times. If you read the books of Thessalonians and 2nd Peter, you will see that when Jesus returns, there will be no more time. That doesn't fit in with Figure 1 below, but Revelation is not about literal time. Revelation is a story of the cause of Christ flourishing and then the cause of Satan seeming to flourish in a repetitive cycle. The non-symbolic books of 1 and 2 Thessalonians and 2 Peter give the end-times picture that tells us that we won't know when Jesus will return until we hear the trumpet blast to end all trumpet blasts. Do not allow the symbolic nature of Revelation to confuse you from the simple and clear message of the passages of the Bible that are not symbolic.

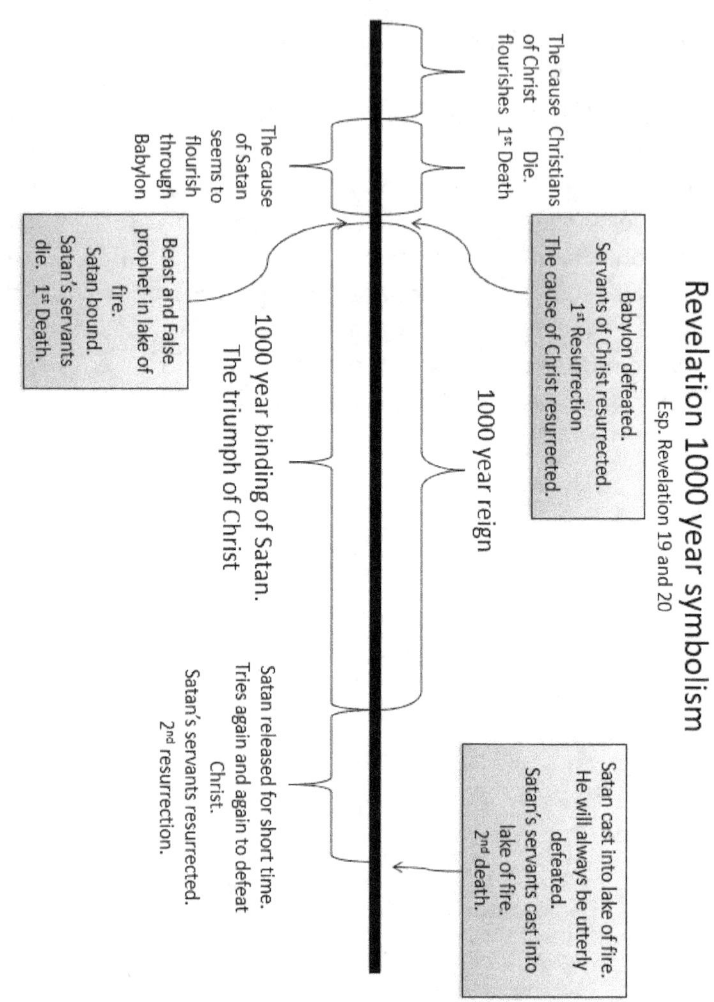

Figure 1: 1000 Year Symbolism

WAR

20:7, When the thousand years are over, Satan will be released from his prison 8, and will go out to deceive the nations in the four corners of the earth—Gog and Magog—and to gather them for battle. In number, they are like the sand on the seashore. 9, They marched across the breadth of the earth and surrounded the camp of God's people, the city he loves. But fire came down from heaven and devoured them. 10, And the devil, who deceived them, was thrown into the lake of burning sulfur, where the beast and the false prophet had been thrown. They will be tormented day and night forever and ever.

Satan, when he is released from his prison, does what Satan does. He goes into the whole earth, deceiving everyone who is willing to be deceived. Although Satan is thoroughly defeated, he has the freedom to continue his efforts to deceive the whole world and turn them against God. As long as God allows time to continue, Satan will continue his efforts against God and His righteous ones. Again, in this battle, we see that Satan doesn't stand a chance. Fire comes down from heaven and consumes all those who were deceived to follow him in battle against the camp of God's people, the church. In this representation of the final battle, Satan is thrown into the lake of burning sulfur, where the beast and the false prophet have already been thrown.

Don't forget that we are seeing a vision that represents something. We are seeing pictures that are meant to teach us something. To understand what we are to learn, let's consider the reference to Gog and Magog. This is a reference to Ezekiel 38 – 39. Ezekiel prophecies that God would bring Gog of the land of Magog with an extremely large army of allies from many lands against Israel. God would bring them against Israel only to defeat them, give Gog a grave in Israel, and destroy the invaders. After that, the fortunes of Israel would be restored. This vision is about the hosts of Satan in the form of Gog and Magog coming against God's people, the church. But instead of victory, Satan suffers total and utter defeat and is thrown into the lake of fire, being tormented forever and ever. In other words, his defeat is complete and irrevocable.

CHAPTER 14

THE CITY OF THE VICTORIOUS

Revelation 20:11 to 22:5.

Now, the final battle is complete. Satan and his allies have been defeated the final time. It is time for the judgment of the unrighteous and the granting of eternal reward to the righteous.

JUDGMENT

20:11 Then I saw a great white throne and him who was seated on it. The earth and the heavens fled from his presence, and there was no place for them. 12 And I saw the dead, great and small, standing before the throne, and books were opened. Another book was opened, which is the book of life. The dead were judged according to what they had done as recorded in the books. 13 The sea gave up the dead that were in it, and death and Hades gave up the dead that were in them, and each person was judged according to what they had done. 14 Then death and Hades were thrown into the lake of fire. The lake of fire is the second death. 15 Anyone whose name was not found written in the book of life was thrown into the lake of fire.

Finally, we see the final judgment. God is on his throne. The physical earth and heaven can't exist in his presence. God fills all in all, so there is no place for the physical universe in this vision! The books of judgment are opened, and they have the evil deeds of all the enemies of God. The Book of Life is opened, which has the righteous deeds of the servants of God. The enemies of God who are in the sea, Death and Hades, are resurrected and face judgment based on their deeds. Anyone not found in the Book of Life is thrown with Death and Hades into the lake of fire. The place represents utter and irrevocable defeat.

As we've observed many times before, Revelation is about heart change. Why not soften your heart, submit to God and his will, and have your name be found in the Book of Life? You get to choose which book your name is found in. God is gracious and wants all people to be saved, but He is also just and will not let the wicked go unpunished. You get to choose which camp you will be found in. Choose wisely.

We must understand that what we see in John's vision is the utter and irrevocable defeat of Satan and the glorious and eternal triumph of Christ. Until God brings the universe to a complete end, Satan will continue to try to defeat Christ and the people of His kingdom, but he will always fail. For those looking for a literal 1000-year reign of Christ on earth, that message is not here in Revelation. To see a clear and concise explanation of the true end-times calendar, see the easy-to-read book by Stafford North, *Like a Thief in the Night*.[CXLIX]

The generally accepted view is that Revelation 20:11-15 is about the final judgment day, and Revelation 21 to 22 are about the church in heaven. We have been reiterating throughout this study that these are representative visions, signs, and symbols, so it would not seem consistent to suddenly abandon that view for a literal view of heaven. The obvious question is if the judgment of the Babylon of the day, Rome, is displayed in such great disasters, why wouldn't the church's victory on earth be displayed in such awesomely great glory? For instance, why would the Holy City, the New Jerusalem, the Bride of Christ, be coming down out of heaven (Revelation 21:2, 9-10) when 1 Thessalonians 4:16-17 tells us that Jesus will come down from heaven to get his bride, which is the church, who will meet him in the air and be taken to be with him forever. This, by the way, refutes the belief of the literal 1000-year physical reign of Christ on earth because Jesus never touches the earth, but everyone meets him in the air. Other arguments that could be raised in favor of this being the victorious church on earth are the kings and nations mentioned in 21:24 and 22:2, the invitation for entrance into the city still being open in 21:6-7, and the need for healing in 22:2.

Add to those arguments the invitation for entrance into the city still being open in 22:14 and 22:17 and the constant reference to things taking place soon.[CL] The arguments from Revelation 22:6 and the following do not apply to the question, "Is this talking about the victorious church on earth or in heaven?" I believe the vision of the victorious church ends at 22:5. The rest is a message to the seven churches about how to apply the whole revelation that they received in John's letter.

Concerning Revelation 22:10, where John is told not to seal up the prophecy because the time is near, in similar language, Daniel was told to seal up a prophecy[CLI] because it was for a time in the distant future. The prophecy of Daniel is about Antiochus Epiphanes and was fulfilled within 380 years of Daniel's writing. The obvious question is that if this is consistent, the revelation of John had to be fulfilled in considerably less than 380 years. How, then, could it be about the church in heaven, which hasn't happened yet?

My question is, why can't both views be true? I believe God is using the picture of glory in heaven to give us the reality of the victorious church on earth. This is a book of visions, signs, and symbols, after all. Both views have issues with man's view of time in a 3-dimensional universe traveling through time. God is outside of time, so maybe we need to stop trying to fit things into a time structure that humans understand.

Now, let's take a closer look at the text. As we do, we will see seven promises and the last two of our seven blessings that are dispersed throughout the book.

A NEW HEAVEN AND A NEW EARTH

21:1 Then I saw "a new heaven and a new earth," for the first heaven and the first earth had passed away, and there was no longer any sea. 2 I saw the Holy City, the new Jerusalem, coming down out of heaven from God, prepared as a bride beautifully dressed for her husband. 3 And I heard a loud voice from the throne saying, "Look! God's dwelling place is now among the people, and he will dwell with them. They will be his people, and God himself will be with them and be their God. 4 He will wipe every tear from their eyes. There will be no more death or mourning or crying or pain, for the old order of things has passed away."

What a wonderful view! Here is the sequence of events I see. When Jesus returns in the clouds of the old heaven, we who are on the old earth will be caught up together with him in the air, [CLII] the old heaven and earth will be destroyed completely, and there will be a new heaven and a new earth, [CLIII] so the bride will come down from the new heaven to the new earth beautifully dressed for her husband! In this new heaven, there is a return to the situation Adam and Eve had before the fall when God made His home with them. They knew no tears, and there was no death, mourning, crying, or pain. We will experience that life eternally. The first promise God gives is of His presence eternally. This leads us to the second promise, which is to experience joy eternally. What could be better than the old order of pain, suffering, and death, mourning and crying having passed way and replaced with getting to dwell with God in the eternal experience of his infinite glory?

THE THRILL OF VICTORY, THE AGONY OF DEFEAT

21:5 He who was seated on the throne said, "I am making everything new!" Then he said, "Write this down, for these words are trustworthy and true." 6 He said to me: "It is done. I am the Alpha and the Omega, the Beginning and the End. To the thirsty I will give water without cost from the spring of the water of life. 7 Those who are victorious will inherit all this, and I will be their God and they will be my children. 8 But the cowardly, the unbelieving, the vile, the murderers, the sexually immoral, those who practice magic arts, the idolaters, and all liars—they will be consigned to the fiery lake of burning sulfur. This is the second death."

God, seated on His throne, is speaking here! "I am making everything new," He says. The new heaven and the new earth have no curse on them, and they, along with those who get to enjoy the water of life, are incorruptible. This is the third promise for all those who do not have to experience the second death - death eternal. The victorious, those who are thirsty for the water of God, the water of life, will receive it at no cost. They get to be God's children in a close relationship with him, crying Abba (daddy), Father, as Jesus did. God's children inherit all the beauty and glory of heaven.

Can we rely on this promise? Is it sure? Have any of the promises of God been unsure? Has He not followed through on every promise He has ever made? If you're unsure about that, read the Bible cover to cover until it is clear to you. That is the message of the Bible – every promise of God is made to happen because God is in control of all things. In His good time, every good promise He has ever made has happened, and those that have not yet come to pass will come to pass because It Is Done! He is the Alpha, the beginning, and the Omega, the end. God starts His purposes and sees them through to the end more surely than evening follows morning.

To those concerned about whether this is talking about the victorious church on earth or in heaven, my answer again is, "Yes." It seems obvious that it could be talking about our home in heaven, but consider that "man shall not live by bread alone, but on every word that proceeds from the mouth of God."[CLIV] The water of life is the word of God, so it is what sustains us both in this life and the next. Let me make my repetitive point again: Revelation is about heart change. Submit to God and be the person to whom these promises belong. Do not rebel and suffer the second death.

21:9 One of the seven angels who had the seven bowls full of the seven last plagues came and said to me, "Come, I will show you the bride, the wife of the Lamb." 10 And he carried me away in the Spirit to a mountain great and high, and showed me the Holy City, Jerusalem, coming down out of heaven from God. 11 It shone with the glory of God, and its brilliance was like that of a very precious jewel, like a jasper, clear as crystal. 12 It had a great, high wall with twelve gates, and with twelve angels at the gates. On the gates were written the names of the twelve tribes of Israel. 13 There were three gates on the east, three on the north, three on the south and three on the west. 14 The wall of the city had twelve foundations, and on them were the names of the twelve apostles of the Lamb. 15 The angel who talked with me had a measuring rod of gold to measure the city, its gates, and its walls. 16 The city was laid out like a square, as long as it was wide. He measured the city with the rod and found it to be 12,000 stadia in length, and as wide and high as it is long. 17 The angel measured the wall using human measurement, and it was 144 cubits thick. 18 The wall was made of jasper, and the city of pure gold, as pure as glass. 19 The foundations of the city walls were decorated with every kind of precious stone. The first foundation was jasper, the second sapphire, the third agate, the fourth emerald, 20 the fifth onyx, the sixth ruby, the seventh chrysolite, the eighth beryl, the ninth topaz, the tenth turquoise, the eleventh jacinth, and the twelfth amethyst. 21 The twelve gates were twelve pearls, each gate made of a single pearl. The great street of the city was of gold, as pure as transparent glass.

The bride that the angel takes John to see is described as the wife of the lamb. But what he sees is the Holy City, Jerusalem. These are the collective people of God, the church, the Holy City, Jerusalem, the bride of Christ, and the wife of the Lamb. The whole picture here is of an incorruptible city – a beautiful home that is safe and secure for those who are victorious. This is the fourth promise for those who are invited to the wedding supper of the Lamb.

If you prefer to view this picture as the victorious church on earth, then we see that the victory and glory have come from God, and the church is protected by the great walls and foundations of the twelve tribes of Israel and the 12 apostles of Christ. If you prefer to view this picture as the victorious church on the new earth, then the coming down out of heaven from God makes sense as it is post-judgment. It is then protected by the twelve tribes of Israel and the 12 apostles of Christ because only those who were faithful to God in whatever era they lived are there.

There is no reason why verse 11 cannot easily fit into either view – the victorious church on earth or the victorious church in heaven. God has given the church His glory. It shines with His brilliance, like a very precious jewel, because that is what the church is to God: A Very Precious Jewel.

I love the song; The Church's One Foundation is Jesus Christ her Lord. Jesus gave the twelve apostles authority to build his church on earth, and through their work, they became the foundation of the church. This is reflected in Jesus' prayer for the church in John 17. In verses 13 through 19, Jesus prayed for the unity of the apostles, then beginning in verse 20, Jesus prayed for those who would believe in Him through their word. Just as Jesus prayed for unity in John 17, we see unity in the twelve foundations of the new city, the twelve gates and angels, and there is unity that the people of God are within the walls and gates of the city.

The rest of the description of the city is there to tell us just how precious it is using human terms. It is measured, indicating that it is completely holy. If you look at the places in scripture where something is measured, it is always set apart for some purpose – usually for a holy purpose. The walls of jasper and the city of the most pure gold speak of its spiritual beauty. The foundations are decorated with every kind of precious stone –

it is holy, precious, beautiful, and costly beyond calculation. The gates are made of huge pearls, one for each gate. This is all so that we can get a picture of God's view of His church. He values it beyond anything we can imagine. He valued it so much that he sent his son, the lamb, to purchase it with his own blood. That is the only price that was sufficient to buy such a valuable item. Imagine what God thinks when you and I devalue the church! His valuation of it is beyond this world!

THE TEMPLE

21:22 I did not see a temple in the city, because the Lord God Almighty and the Lamb are its temple. 23 The city does not need the sun or the moon to shine on it, for the glory of God gives it light, and the Lamb is its lamp. 24 The nations will walk by its light, and the kings of the earth will bring their splendor into it. 25 On no day will its gates ever be shut, for there will be no night there. 26 The glory and honor of the nations will be brought into it. 27 Nothing impure will ever enter it, nor will anyone who does what is shameful or deceitful, but only those whose names are written in the Lamb's book of life.

Imagine not needing a temple, church building, or any other building to draw close to God. Imagine having all the light you could ever want without the sun, moon, stars, or some manufactured lighting system. Imagine having the light of God's glory through the lamp of the Lamb. This is the true spiritual nature of the victorious church on earth and in heaven. The nations on earth will walk by the light of the church. Isn't that so true? Don't you see that in our world? How dark would our world be if it were not enlightened by those who preach God's word in their lives and influence those who do not know the Lord and the impact He would have on their lives? Consider how much more devastating wars and conflicts would be on earth if not for the calming and blessing influence of believers.

While verse 24 seems to fit the church on earth better, verses 25 – 27 seem to fit the heavenly version better. But either way, the church is only for the saved – those who have been baptized by faith into Christ. Scripture says that it is those people who are added to the church. As such, nothing impure enters the church. No one who does what is shameful or deceitful will enter the church. It does not mean that those who enter have never been impure or done what is shameful or deceitful. All have, but they have been washed. They have been cleansed. They have been forgiven, and their names are written in the Lamb's Book of Life.

THE RIVER

22:1 Then the angel showed me the river of the water of life, as clear as crystal, flowing from the throne of God and of the Lamb 2 down the middle of the great street of the city. On each side of the river stood the tree of life, bearing twelve crops of fruit, yielding its fruit every month. And the leaves of the tree are for the healing of the nations. 3 No longer will there be any curse. The throne of God and of the Lamb will be in the city, and his servants will serve him. 4 They will see his face, and his name will be on their foreheads. 5 There will be no more night. They will not need the light of a lamp or the light of the sun, for the Lord God will give them light. And they will reign for ever and ever.

There is a river in this amazing cube-shaped city. The waters of life flow through this city from what source? From the throne of God! In Revelation 21:3, we see that God's place is now among the people (the church), and he will dwell with them. Revelation 21:5 says that He who sits on the throne (God) said, "I am making everything new." Now we see a wonderful thing. That throne is within the walls of that amazing city that has come down out of heaven from the one who sits on the throne within the city. Remember, the city is the bride of the Lamb, the church – God's dwelling is truly among his people! Amazing! Wonderful!

The water of the river gives constant life to the people of the city, and it causes the tree of life to grow and bear fruit every month. Wait. How will there be seasons and months if there is no night? Now we're back to wording, which makes sense if we're talking about the victorious church on earth. It appears that the water is the word of God. And I would add that the water is the worship of God and the fellowship of Christians with each other and with God. The Tree of Life is the word of God that gives us life through whatever circumstances try to steal our lives. When we are worshiping God in spirit and truth, do we not see the face of the Lamb? When we study the Bible together in honesty and with an earnest desire to grow in the knowledge and unity of the Godhead, do we not see the face of Christ? Is his name not written on our hearts and our foreheads, clearly for others to see? Are we not enlightened with the Light of God and Christ in these things? God is light, and in him, there is no darkness at all.^{CLV}

In verse four, we see our fifth promise – to see the face of God. That is amazing. Consider what God told Moses. In Exodus 33, Moses sets up a tent and calls it the Tabernacle of Meeting. The Lord spoke to Moses face to face as a man would speak to his friend (verse 11). In verse 18, Moses asks God to show him His glory. God says, "I will make all My goodness pass before you," but "You cannot see My face; for no man shall see me and live." I suggest that you read the whole chapter. God spoke to Moses face to face in some spiritual way, but even Moses was not allowed to see God's face. The promise we have here in Revelation 22:4 is that we will go beyond what even Moses was able to do and see God's face! Moses was God's friend, and he couldn't see God's face. We will see God's face and be in the category of God's friends.

We have the promise of getting our light from God and reigning forever and ever – not just for 1000 years. The 1000-year symbolic timeframe was clearly on earth, so the reign described here as being forever and ever may add to the argument for this, picturing the victorious church in heaven.

CHAPTER 15

OMEGA

Revelation 22:6 to 22:21

The vision is now over. Now, we are back to John's present day. We now get to look at the final conversation that John has with the angel that Jesus sent and with Jesus himself.

JESUS IS COMING SOON

22:6 The angel said to me, "These words are trustworthy and true. The Lord, the God who inspires the prophets, sent his angel to show his servants the things that must soon take place." 7 "Look, I am coming soon! Blessed is the one who keeps the words of the prophecy written in this scroll." 8 I, John, am the one who heard and saw these things. And when I had heard and seen them, I fell down to worship at the feet of the angel who had been showing them to me. 9 But he said to me, "Don't do that! I am a fellow servant with you and with your fellow prophets and with all who keep the words of this scroll. Worship God!" 10 Then he told me, "Do not seal up the words of the prophecy of this scroll, because the time is near. 11 Let the one who does wrong continue to do wrong; let the vile person continue to be vile; let the one who does right continue to do right; and let the holy person continue to be holy."

Before Jesus speaks, the angel who is working with John reminds him that all the words of God are trustworthy and true. The same God who inspires the prophets also sent this angel to show his servants what must soon take place. Then Jesus says, "I am coming soon." The angel then tells John not to seal up the words of the scroll because the time is near. Referring to chapter 2 of this book, we notice that the words to Daniel were "seal up the words of the prophecy" because they refer to a distant time — a time only 380 years in the future. Many people have many opinions about what this revelation is about, including the fall of Rome. But Rome did not fall until 476 AD. If, as we asserted, Revelation had been written in AD 95, then the fulfillment would have been the same 380-year difference! How could 380 years both be the distant future for Daniel and soon for the seven churches? Still, others assert that the events pictured in Revelation have not yet happened. How can either of these views be tenable based on the command of verse 10 above?

My assertion is that the purpose of this book, Revelation, is to change the heart. This book was written specifically for seven churches in existence around AD 95, and we get to listen in. Whatever the events depicted in Revelation must have been experienced by the generation living at the time. Jesus' final return has not yet happened. We know this because when he does return, this universe will pass away, immediately followed by judgment. Since, if you're reading this, Jesus' final return is yet in the future, we may also experience the events depicted in Revelation, and we must heed the same cautions that God gave those to whom Revelation was addressed.

John falls at the angel's feet to worship. Maybe he was confused by the words of Jesus, saying he would be coming soon, and mistook the angel for Jesus. Is that possible? In any case, John was worshipping the wrong being, and the Angel was unwilling to accept any of the glory that belonged to the Lord. Only God is worthy of worship – worship Him only. An angel is a fellow servant with the apostles and the prophets, neither of which has been physically with us since early in the second century AD. But the angel is also a fellow servant to God with all those who keep the words of Revelation. That might include you! Are you keeping the words of Revelation? It requires the God-ordained heart change to do so.

Let the one who does wrong continue to do wrong. Why would God tell us that? While it might be debatable if the things written from chapters 21 to 22, verse 5, are about the victorious city on earth or in heaven, it seems that Revelation 21:6 and the following are about how we should live now until victory is complete. It is not my responsibility to change someone's actions. It is my responsibility to share the gospel with them and lead them through God's word as far as they are willing to go. If they choose to continue to do wrong or live a vile life, there is nothing I can or should do about it. But the righteous and holy person is encouraged to continue to be righteous and holy.

THE ALPHA AND THE OMEGA

22:12 "Look, I am coming soon! My reward is with me, and I will give to each person according to what they have done. 13 I am the Alpha and the Omega, the First and the Last, the Beginning and the End. 14 "Blessed are those who wash their robes, that they may have the right to the tree of life and may go through the gates into the city. 15 Outside are the dogs, those who practice magic arts, the sexually immoral, the murderers, the idolaters and everyone who loves and practices falsehood. 16 "I, Jesus, have sent my angel to give you this testimony for the churches. I am the Root and the Offspring of David, and the bright Morning Star." 17 The Spirit and the bride say, "Come!" And let the one who hears say, "Come!" Let the one who is thirsty come; and let the one who wishes take the free gift of the water of life.

Again, we see Jesus, who began all things, say that he is coming soon to end all things. Perhaps it would be better translated as coming quickly, which could, in that case, mean that whenever he comes, it won't be some long-drawn-out process. It will seem very sudden to those who are alive when he comes. What is more important is that He brings his reward for us with him. His reward is based on what we have done. It only makes sense for me to do the things that will enable Jesus to bring a reward that I would be happy to receive. That is what this whole book is about. Revelation is encouraging and motivating us to put away the deeds of darkness, to wash our robes and make them gleaming white in the blood of the Lamb.

That way, I will have the right to enter that great city, eat from the Tree of Life, and live forever.

Even while we remain on earth, we are experiencing the safety of being in Christ and in his holy city, his bride, and the church. Outside the church are the dogs, those who practice magic arts, those who practice sexual immorality, those who murder, those who put other things above their obedience and loyalty to God, and those who love and practice falsehood. Wait, do you mean to say that if I go to a palm reader I may be choosing to be outside the church? Yes. If I choose to engage in sex outside of marriage, sex with someone of my same gender, any kind of sex that is not within the marriage of one man and one woman? Yes. If I choose to abort my baby or help someone commit suicide? Yes. Do I want to live in a God-pleasing and eternity-enhancing way? Then, I need to put all those selfish ways away from me.

If you remember back to the very beginning of Revelation, we noticed that this is a revelation of Jesus. Here now, Jesus identifies himself. He is the Root of David - the Alpha, and the Offspring of David — the Omega. Jesus sent the angel to give testimony for the churches — the churches in 95 AD, not only for them but for the church today as well. Jesus, along with the angel, the Spirit, and the bride, invite all to come into the city. The bride is the city. The bride is the church. This is an invitation to come to Christ and be added to his church by God. Everyone who hears the invitation should also invite everyone else to come into the city. Everyone who gives up evil outside the city and washes their robes can come into the city and drink the water of life. The existence outside the city should make you very thirsty! Let go of all the things in the world that seem so attractive yet leave you dry and thirsty. Repent of those things and put your faith in Christ. Wash your robes in the blood of the Lamb by being immersed in the water of baptism through faith in the power of God to raise you from the death of sin, just as his power raised Jesus from the death of crucifixion.

AMEN. COME, LORD JESUS

22:18 I warn everyone who hears the words of the prophecy of this scroll: If anyone adds anything to them, God will add to that person the plagues described in this scroll. 19 And if anyone takes words away from this scroll of prophecy, God will take away from that person any share in the tree of life and in the Holy City, which are described in this scroll. 20 He who testifies to these things says, "Yes, I am coming soon." Amen. Come, Lord Jesus. 21 The grace of the Lord Jesus be with God's people. Amen.

What can I say about this? Only that I hope that I did not add anything to the words of this prophecy or take anything away from them. I certainly had no intention of doing so. This summarizes the whole purpose of Revelation, doesn't it? We are given a picture that goes deep into our subconscious and drives us away from the things that will keep us from eternal life.

This is a revelation of Jesus, and Jesus testifies to its truth. He is coming soon. Amen. Come, Lord Jesus! Until he does come, his grace is with those who are God's people. Please accept his grace by obeying the gospel so that you can honestly look forward to his coming.

PROMISES AND BLESSINGS

Jesus had promised (verse 6) to come to save his people from the oppression that the world brings in whatever era they live. Every oppressor comes to a sudden end. He promises us (verse 21) that his grace will always be with us, who are God's people. These promises apply to those who have received his blessings. Who is blessed? Verse 7 says those who keep the words of Revelation, and verse 14 says those who wash their robes. We've discussed throughout this book what those things mean and how to do them. Let us, with intention, put into our hearts those things which will drive us away from unrighteousness and toward righteousness so we can find ourselves pleasing to God.

A Final Word

Much of the fear that keeps people from reading the Book of Revelation is the unfamiliar symbolism, grotesque creatures, and scary events. Many people get overwhelmed and disoriented by all these things. These are the very things that should attract you to the book because of the purpose it serves.

The purpose of the emotional trip Revelation takes you through is to motivate you. It uses the strongest part of how we are created to move us from sin to righteousness.

I hope that reading this book has given you a better understanding of Revelation and that meditating on its message has given you a closer connection to God. I also hope that you have greater confidence in your salvation or were led to salvation through baptism by faith in the saving power of Jesus' sacrifice. I hope that you have a stronger desire to share God's saving message with others.

STUDY GUIDE

Questions for thought and discussion

Preface

Questions

1. What two concerns do people have today regarding Revelation that were not concerns for the original recipients?
2. What is the main purpose of Revelation?

Chapter 1 - Method

Objectives

1. Present the method of interpretation used by this book to share the message of Revelation.
2. Present the interactive method that Revelation uses to help us grow.

Questions

1. How are most of our actions decided, logically or emotionally? Provide a scripture reference that supports your answer.
2. What strategy is suggested to connect your emotional and logical thoughts?
3. How is prayer a tool to connect logic and emotion?
4. Why are your prayers important to God?

Chapter 2 – Alpha - Revelation 1:1 To 1:4

Objectives

1. Discover Revelation's who, what, when, how, and why.
2. Prepare ourselves for the themes that we will experience.

Questions

1. What type of literature is Revelation, and how should we read the book?
2. What was John's commission? To whom was he commissioned? What is their significance?
3. What is the source and lineage of John's message? What is the importance of this lineage?
4. What reference to time is repeated numerous times in Revelation? How do we understand this reference?
5. How does Revelation reveal its message? Why is this important?
6. How many blessings are given in Revelation? Why is that number significant?
7. Consider the themes of Revelation and allow them to inspire you to greater faith and obedience.

Chapter 3 – A Wonderful Savior - Revelation 1:5 To 1:20

Objectives

1. Discover God's power and His wonderful Savior.
2. Discover God's protection of His church.
3. Discover the Wonderful Savior moments in the text.

Questions

1. Revelation is a book to be ___________ more than ___________. Why is that?
2. What is the blessing spoken of in these verses? Who gives the blessing? Why are they described as they are?
3. What do we learn from the hymns of praise that are being sung? Can we join in on these hymns today?
4. In what ways does John relate to his readers spiritually?
5. How do you feel about the three things in which John was partnered with his readers?
6. What do you think of the loud voice that John heard? Do you think loud voices will be a common thing in Revelation?

7. When John turned around, what did he see? What do they represent, and what is important about how they are described?

8. Who did John see, and what is important about how he is described?

9. What do the seven stars in Jesus' right hand represent? What happened to them when Jesus touched John? Does that tell you anything about how Jesus feels about you?

10. Find at least 25 descriptions of our wonderful God and Savior in this chapter.

Chapter 4 – A Church Under Pressure - Revelation 2:1 To 3:22

Objectives

1. Discover the overall message to the churches.
2. Discover the application for us.

Questions

1. The letter to each church is addressed to whom?
2. What is the pattern of the messages to the churches?
3. How is Jesus described for each church? How does Jesus' description relate to the message?
4. With what command does each message conclude? What can we learn from this?
5. What is promised to those who overcome?
6. Compare the first four churches. What is the difference in their doctrinal purity?
7. Compare the last three churches. What is different in their Spirituality?
8. Can we learn anything from the similarity in the description of Jesus to the churches of Ephesus and Sardis?

Chapter 5 – The Throne of God - Revelation 4:1 to 5:14

Objectives

1. Observe the worship of God.
2. Observe the worship of Jesus.
3. Take your time and meditate on these thoughts.

Questions

1. What is the significance of the open door in heaven?
2. What does "After this" mean?
3. What does John mean by "I was in the Spirit"?
4. Where is the throne of God? How often is the throne of God mentioned in the Revelation? What does the throne and its location signify?
5. What is the appearance of the one on the throne? What impression does that give you?
6. Where is the rainbow? What does it look like? What does it signify?
7. Who are the 24 elders? How are they dressed, and what does this signify?
8. What are the seven lamps?
9. What is before the throne? What is it for?
10. What is coming from the throne? How does that make you feel?
11. Who or what are the 4 creatures?
12. What do we learn about the worship of God?
13. What did God have in his right hand?
14. Why did John weep? Why should he not weep?
15. Who is able (and worthy) to open the scroll? Why?
16. What was the appearance of the Lamb? What does his appearance signify?
17. Where is the Lamb standing? Where are the seven spirits?
18. What were the creatures and elders holding? What were they singing?
19. Who else was singing? What were they singing?

20. What is the third group to sing? What is their song?

21. Why are we shown this glorious worship? What purpose does it serve?

Chapter 6 – The Scroll and Seven Seals - Revelation 6:1 to 8:5

Objectives

1. Discover God's ready judgment on evil and oppression.

2. Discover who can stand in the midst of God's judgment.

3. Discover our purpose and God's care.

Questions

1. What command is given with the opening of each of the first four seals? Who gives the command, and to whom is it given?

2. Describe each horse.

3. What do the four horses represent?

4. What does John see and hear after the opening of the fifth seal? Does this change your opinion about what the four horses represent?

5. What happens when the Sixth seal is opened? Is this referring to Jesus' second coming? Why or why not? What question does the chapter end with?

6. What power do the four angels have? What are they holding? What command did they receive?

7. Who are the 144,000? What is the seal on the 144,000?

8. Is 144,000 a literal number? Are there precisely 12,000 sealed from each of the 12 tribes listed?

9. Where is the multitude standing? How are they dressed? What are they holding?

10. Who joins the multitude in the second volley of worship?

11. How is the multitude identified by one of the elders? What is their purpose and blessing?

12. What events take place when the seventh seal is opened? What is their significance?

Chapter 7 – The Seven Trumpets - Revelation 8:6 to 11:19

Objectives

1. Observe God's call to repentance.

2. Discover God's commitment to his covenant with his people.

3. Discover God's judgment on those who would hurt God's people.

Questions

1. For what are trumpets used?

2. Describe what happens when each of the first four trumpets is sounded. How do you interpret these events?

3. How many "woes" did the eagle announce were to come? Who are the inhabitants of the earth?

4. Describe the vision of the fifth trumpet. What is the point?

5. Describe the vision of the sixth trumpet. What is the point?

6. Describe the Angel. What does he swear? What is he holding? What do you think these things indicate?

7. What is the significance of Measuring the Temple?

8. Who are the two witnesses? What events occur? What does this mean?

9. What events accompany the Seventh Trumpet? What do they signify?

10. What is the point of the temple and ark in heaven?

Chapter 8 – The Seven-Headed Dragon - Revelation 12:1 to 12:17

Objectives

1. Discover Satan's hate of Christ and the Church.

2. Discover God's victory over Satan.

3. Discover Satan's response to being defeated.

Questions

1. Describe the woman. What does this tell us about her? What are the possibilities as to her identity?

2. Describe the Dragon. Who or what is represented?

3. What gender was the child born to the woman? Where did the child go? Who is this?

4. Where did the woman go? What is pictured here?

5. Who declares war against the dragon? What two names are given to the dragon?

6. What four things have "Now come"? Can you point to a specific time when this takes place?

7. What are the weapons of those who overcome?

8. What event in the Old Testament sounds like the happenings in 12:13-16?

9. Who are the rest of the offspring?

Chapter 9 – The Two Beasts - Revelation 13:1 to 13:18

Objectives

1.   Discover Satan's use of corrupt government.

2.   Discover Satan's false prophet.

3.   Discover the meaning of Satan's mark.

Questions

1.   Where did this beast come from? What does the fatal wound that was healed remind you of?

2.   What did the sea beast receive from the Dragon, and for what purpose?

3.   How did the sea beast affect the "whole world"?

4.   What does the picture of the sea beast signify?

5.   What admonition is given to the saints?

6.   Where did the second beast come from? How is its appearance different from the dragon and the sea beast?

7.   What was the source of the land beast's authority? What did he do with it, and for what purpose?

8.   What does the picture of the land beast signify?

9.   Who received the mark of the beast, and for what purpose?

10. What is the mark of the beast, and what point is being made by it?

Chapter 10 – The Seven Voices - Revelation 14:1 to 14:20

Objectives

1.   Identify the 144,000.

2.   Be encouraged by a message of hope.

Questions

1.   What is the first thing John sees in Revelation 14? Why do you think that is? What is the significance of "Standing on Mount Zion"?
2.   How are the 144,000 Described? What were they (the first voice) singing?
3.   If we take the 144,000 literally, what else in this context must we take literally? Is there an alternative?
4.   What did the first angel (the second voice) say?
5.   The second angel (the third voice) proclaimed the destruction of what nation?
6.   What does the third angel (the fourth voice) say will happen to the worshipers of the beast?
7.   Where did the fifth voice come from? Who is blessed and why?
8.   Who spoke as the sixth voice? To whom did he speak? Who was harvested?
9.   The seventh voice called for what harvest in 14:17-20? What is different about this harvest from the one in 14:14-16?

Chapter 11 – The Seven Bowls - Revelation 15:1 to 16:21

Objectives

1.   Observe the song of God's victorious people.

2.   Discover the pouring out of God's judgment.

3.   Discover God's continuing call to repentance.

Questions

1.   What sign did John see in 15:1?

2.   Where did the victors stand? In what two ways is their song identified? Why do they have harps?

3. Where did the seven angels come from? What significance does this have?

4. What effect did the first two bowls have? To what extent was the damage?

5. Where did the third angel pour his judgment? What was the response of the angel in charge of that area?

6. Where was the judgment of the fourth and fifth angels poured? What was the purpose of this judgment?

7. What happened to the Euphrates River when the sixth bowl was poured out? What does this signify?

8. What blessing is pronounced here? What does it mean for one to "keep his clothes with him"?

9. Where was the 7th plague poured, and what was its result? What is different about this plague than the fourth and fifth plagues?

Chapter 12 – The Prostitute - Revelation 17:1 to 18:24

Objectives

1. Identify the prostitute.

2. Identify the beast.

3. Observe the fall of an empire.

Questions

1. What is the description and identity of the woman?

2. What is the description and beast? How are the seven heads identified?

3. What identity is given to the ten horns and to the water?

4. What do you make of the beast and ten horns destroying the prostitute?

5. What was the Angel's message?

6. What does the angel's description tell us about his message?

7. What is the call to God's people? Is it applicable to us today?

8. How do you interpret 18:6, 7?

9. What three categories of people mourned her loss?

10. Where did they stand? What does this signify?

11. Who is rejoicing? Why?

12. How was Babylon's fall described? Why? Can we relate this to our life and situation?

Chapter 13 – The Rider - Revelation 19:1 to 20:10

Objectives

1. Observe the worship of the righteous.

2. Identify the rider on the white horse.

3. Identify the 1000-year reign.

Questions

1. What prompted the rejoicing in 19:1-8?

2. How was the bride made ready? Who is invited to the wedding supper?

3. What do you make of John falling down to worship the angel?

4. Explain the statement, "For the testimony of Jesus is the spirit of prophecy."

5. Who is the rider on the white horse? What is he called? Why does verse 12 say, "he has a name written on him that no one knows but he himself"?

6. What do you make of this supper described in 19:17-21?

7. What did all the armies that were with Jesus do?

8. What was different about the fate of the beast & false prophet from those who had been deluded by them?

9. Where was the dragon put? When does this happen? How long was his sentence? What happens when his term is up?

10. What is the dragon unable to do? What does this signify?

11. Who was resurrected? Who remains dead? For what period?

12. Is this the same 1000 years as vs 1-3? What does the 1000 years signify?

13. What does Satan do when released from prison? What do these things signify?

Chapter 14 – The City of the Victorious - Revelation 20:11 to 22:5

Objectives

1. Identify the New Jerusalem

2. Discover five of the seven promises to the church

3. Be encouraged to keep on keeping on.

Questions

1. Who is resurrected in 20:11-15? What happens to them?

2.   What promise are we given in 21:1-3?

3.   What is the second promise we are given?

4.   What is the third promise?

5.   How is the bride described?

6.   How is the city described?

7.   What is the fourth promise that is contained in these verses?

8.   What is the fifth promise that is given in 22:4-5?

Chapter 15 – Omega - Revelation 20:11 to 22:5

Objectives

1.   Discover the last two promises to the church

2.   Be encouraged to keep on keeping on.

Questions

1.   What is the sixth promise?

2.   Who is blessed in 22:7, 14? How do we accomplish this?

3.   What is meant by 22:11?

4.   What is the seventh promise?

END NOTES

Preface

[I] James Burton Coffman, *Commentary on Revelation* (Firm Foundation Publishing House 1979)

[II] Some of the commentaries I have referenced.

       a. Ibid
       b. Christopher A. Davis, *The College Press NIV Commentary Revelation* (College Press 2000)
       c. Jim McGuiggan, *Revelation* (Montex 1976)
       d. G.R. Beasley-Murray, *The Eerdmans Bible Commentary* (Eerdmans 1970)
       e. Dan Winkler, *The Church at Home with God* (Winkler Publications 2006)

Chapter 1 Method

[III] Vince Poscente, *The Ant and the Elephant: Leadership for the Self* (Be Invincible Group 2004)

[IV] Revelation 8:3-5, Notice the prayers of the saints were offered on the altar before God with incense in verse 3 and then those same contents were hurled to the earth from which were sounded the seven trumpets.

Chapter 2 Alpha

[V] Christopher A. Davis, *The College Press NIV Commentary Revelation* (College Press 2000), pages 61-63.

[VI] James Burton Coffman, *Commentary on Revelation* (Firm Foundation Publishing House 1979), pages 3-7.

[VII] Revelation 22:18-19

[VIII] James Burton Coffman, *James Burton Coffman Commentaries Galatians, Ephesians, Philippians, and Colossians* (A. C. U. Press 1977), page 68.

[IX] Matthew 16:17

[X] Galatians 3:19b

[XI] Galatians 3:16-17, 19a, 23-25

[XII] Revelation 2:16, 3:11, 11:14, 22:6, 7, 10, 12, 20.

[XIII] Vine's Expository Dictionary of Biblical Words (Nelson 1985)

[XIV] Strong's Lexicon (https://biblehub.com/greek/4394.htm)

[XV] See Revelation 1:3 and 22:7

[XVI] Vine's Expository Dictionary of Biblical Words (Nelson 1985)

[XVII] Strong's Lexicon (https://biblehub.com/greek/3466.htm)

[XVIII] See Revelation 1:20, 10:7, 17:5, and 17:7

[XIX] Strong's Lexicon (https://biblehub.com/greek/602.htm)

[XX] See Revelation 1:9, 2:3,10,22, 3:10, 9:5, 13:10, and 14:12

[XXI] See Revelation 6:10, 16:15, 18:8,20, 19:11, and 20:11-13

[XXII] See Revelation 4:8-11, 5:9-14, 7:10-12, 15:3,4, 16:5-7, and 19:1-8

[XXIII] See Ephesians 1:20

Chapter 3 A Wonderful Savior

[XXIV] Stafford North, *Like a Thief in the Night* (21st Century Christian 2015)

[XXV] 1 John 5:21

[XXVI] Colossians 2:9-15

[XXVII] https://www.britannica.com/technology/bronze-alloy

[XXVIII] Dan Winkler, *The Church at Home with God* (Winkler Publications 2006)

Chapter 4 A Church under Pressure

[XXIX] James Burton Coffman, *Commentary on Revelation* (Firm Foundation Publishing House 1979).

[XXX] See Revelation 2:16

[XXXI] See Revelation 1:16

[XXXII] See 1 Kings 18-21

[XXXIII] See Matthew 10:1

[XXXIV] 2 Peter 2:19

[XXXV] Revelation 22:16

[XXXVI] Colossians 1:27

[XXXVII] Revelation 3:20

[XXXVIII] Revelation 2:2

[XXXIX] Revelation 2:9

[XL] Revelation 2:14-15

[XLI] Revelation 2:20

[XLII] Matthew 12:7

[XLIII] Revelation 3:1b

[XLIV] Revelation 3:8

[XLV] Revelation 3:15-16

[XLVI] Jim McGuiggan, *Revelation* (Montex 1976) page 47.

[XLVII] James Burton Coffman, *Commentary on Revelation* (Firm Foundation Publishing House 1979) page 50.

XLVIII See also Ephesians 6:17 and Hebrews 4:12

XLIX See also Hebrews 4:13

L Isaiah 11:2

Chapter 5 The Throne of God

LI 1 Samuel 4:4

LII Psalm 2:4

LIII Psalm 7:7

LIV Psalm 9:11

LV Isaiah 40:22

LVI 2 Chronicles 18:18

LVII Canva.com

LVIII Christopher A. Davis, *The College Press NIV Commentary Revelation* (College Press 2000) Page 164.

LIX Revelation 3:4-5

LX Revelation 2:26 27

LXI Exodus 39:30

LXII 2 Corinthians 4:17

LXIII Isaiah 6:1-3

LXIV Ezekiel 1 and 10

LXV 1 Chronicles 28:18

LXVI Revelation 4:5

LXVII Revelation 1:13

LXVIII John 16:33

Chapter 6 The Scroll and Seven Seals

LXIX See Matthew 24:6-7, Mark 13:7-8 and Luke 21:9-11.

LXX Ezekiel 14:12-23. See especially verses 13, 15, 17, 19, and 21.

LXXI Zechariah 6:1-8

LXXII (Revelation, Truth Commentaries p. 87)

LXXIII Ephesians 5:10

LXXIV Ezekiel 9:1-6

LXXV Ezekiel 21:3-4

LXXVI Jim McGuiggan, *Revelation* (Montex 1976) pages 107, 111

LXXVII 2 Timothy 2:19

LXXVIII Hebrews 7:25

LXXIX Romans 1:16

LXXX Romans 6:1ff

LXXXI 1 John 1:7

Chapter 7 The Seven Trumpets

LXXXII Jeremiah 51:24-26

LXXXIII Isaiah 14:3-15

LXXXIV Romans 10:14-15

LXXXV 2 Timothy 2:22

LXXXVI Revelation 7:1

LXXXVII Revelation 6:12-14; 8:1

LXXXVIII Revelation 9:13-19; 11:15

LXXXIX Ezekiel 40-43

XC Romans 11:25-27

XCI Genesis 19

XCII Exodus 7:1

XCIII 1 Peter 2:9

XCIV Revelation 9:21

XCV Revelation 11:13

Chapter 8 The Seven Headed Dragon

XCVI Psalm 89:17

XCVII Galatians 3:26-27, Ephesians 2:4-7, Revelation 5:10

XCVIII Jude 1:9

XCIX Daniel 10:13, 10:21, 12:1

C Genesis 3

CI Daniel 10:10-14

CII 2 Thessalonians 1:8

CIII 1 John 5:13

CIV Jim McGuiggan, *Revelation* (Montex 1976) page 167

Chapter 9 The Two Beasts

CV Isaiah 57:20

CVI Revelation 17:15

CVII Revelation 6:12-17

CVIII Revelation 16:13, 19:20, and 20:10

Chapter 10 The Seven Voices

CIX Revelation 12:11,12a

CX Psalm 2:6

CXI Romans 11:26, 27; Acts 1:8

CXII I Corinthians 15:20-23

CXIII Jim McGuiggan, *Revelation* (Montex 1976) page 206

CXIV Genesis 17:5

CXV Vince Poscente, *The Ant and the Elephant: Leadership for the Self* (Be Invincible Group 2004) page 61

CXVI "Ironic," by Alanis Morissette, Jagged Little Pill, Maveric, 1995, track 10

CXVII Revelation 13:17

CXVIII Revelation 1:9 and following

CXIX Revelation 5:6-7

CXX Revelation 7:17

CXXI Revelation 14:1

CXXII Revelation 10:6

CXXIII Hebrews 13:11-13

CXXIV Revelation 11:1-2

Chapter 11 The Seven Bowls

CXXV Revelation 12:1-2

CXXVI Daniel 5:30-31

CXXVII Revelation 7:14

CXXVIII Exodus 28:36-38

CXXIX Exodus 24:17

CXXX Proverbs 24:4-5

CXXXI Exodus 25:9,40; Hebrews 8:5

CXXXII Revelation 3:12, 7:15, 11:1-2

CXXXIII Exodus 40:33-35

CXXXIV Numbers 16:42

CXXXV 1 Kings 8:10-11, 2 Chronicles 5:13-14

CXXXVI Exodus 9:1-12

CXXXVII Revelation 6:9-11

CXXXVIII 1 Samuel 31:8

CXXXIX 2 Chronicles 35:20-27

CXL "Little Sister," by Jewel, Pieces of You, Atlantic, 1995, track 3

Chapter 12 The Prostitute

CXLI Isaiah 23

CXLII Ezekiel 16, 23

CXLIII Exodus 34:33-34; 2 Corinthians 3:13

CXLIV Matthew 24:15-18

CXLV 2 Peter 3:10-11

CXLVI Revelation 14:3

CXLVII John 12:48

CXLVIII Revelation 17:8

CXLIX Stafford North, *Like a Thief in the Night* (21st Century Christian 2015)

[CL] Revelation 22:6, 7, 10, 12, and 20
[CLI] Daniel 8:26
[CLII] 1 Thessalonians 4:16-17
[CLIII] 2 Peter 3:10-13
[CLIV] Matthew 4:4
[CLV] 1 John 1:5